"It is so refreshing to see a book that takes the effects of bullying seriously and deals with them so sensitively."

THE
LAUNDROMAT

a memoir

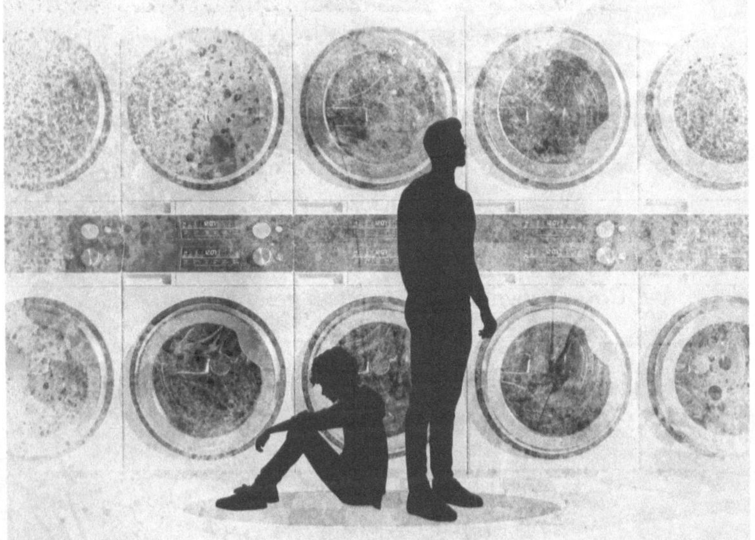

NICK RATO

with Ben Jeapes

THE LAUNDROMAT

Published by Nick Rato.

© 2025 Nick Rato.

ISBN 979-8-9997606-0-9

Editing and interior design:
Ben Jeapes
www.benjeapes.com

Cover design coordination and proofreading:
Lydia Jenkins
www.lgjenkins.com/services

Cover design:
100 Covers
100covers.com

www.nickrato.com

I dedicate this book to my son, my daughter, my Barney, and my wife. You are all my life. I thank God for each and every one of you, every day, every night.
Love, Dad.

CHAPTER 1

I turn my back on the rain lashing against the window. My face is wet enough already. It's like those machine gun pellets of water want to get in and join in the fun. Amelia is fast asleep in her own little world, with our Maltese, Barney, curled up at the foot of the bed. The kids are sleeping in their rooms.

Some mornings I just wake up like this. I open my eyes and it all comes crashing in with dawn's early light. Who am I, what am I, what am I doing, what is my life all about? All I know is that I am always upset. With the world, with my family, with everything. And on a morning like this, when a storm has come raging down Long Island Sound and the heavens have opened, my mood can be ten times as dark.

So I will lighten it with a little spontaneity. I'll make a cup of tea, leave it by her bedside. Maybe wake her with a gentle kiss. Mr. Romantic, that's me.

I slip my robe on, and wipe my eyes on the sleeve, and head for the door.

Down the hallway, in the kitchen ahead, I hear voices. I was wrong, the kids are up. And straightaway my mood lifts.

They are my life, that boy and girl. Boy and girl? They would say, "Man and woman, thanks, Dad." And fair enough. Handsome Daniel, dark and Italian like me, is twenty-five and getting his master's degree to become a PE teacher. Beautiful Miranda, slender and brunette like her Mom, is twenty-four and she's starting a PhD in nursing in September. Maybe they're both a bit older than usual to be living with their parents still, but let's be realistic, Amelia and I are cheaper than commercial landlords.

Boy and girl, man and woman, they are still my life and just the thought of them can cheer me up. Screw the rain outside, there's still a little sunshine in my heart.

They are joshing each other as I reach the door.

"Hey, doofus, you left the jar top off again."

"Say, you know it takes peanut butter more than like thirty seconds to dry out, don't you?"

They are each other's best friends. They can talk to each other like that because they are just so relaxed with each other. What two solid human beings my wife has raised. Two great adults who are very responsible and both working hard towards their future. I love them so much.

"That's not the point. When peanut butter goes hard it's impossible to spread properly..."

I can hear the smiles in their voices.

"Meh, just slap some of your moisturizer on it..."

I push the door open and my heart breaks.

I might prefer it if they just switched to scowling when they saw me. At least that would be honest. But the smiles stay. It's just the light behind them that goes out. The smiles are fixed, frozen, but the animating joy behind them has vanished.

"Oh, hi, Dad." Daniel recovers first. Slice of toast halfway to his mouth. Still smiling. "Did we wake you up?"

I pretend absolutely nothing unusual has happened.

"No, I guess that was the weather. Our window faces the wind so the rain really hammers on it." I go over to the cupboard, fetch a cup, drop the teabag into it.

"Oh, okay." And they try to hide the relief but they can't. I know them too well. It's like they sag down just a millimeter as they relax, but I see it.

I keep my back to them while I fill the cup up from the hot water tap, so they can't see my eyes starting to brim again. The boiling water hisses and splutters while they make fake conversation. By the time I've squeezed the bag out and put it in the garbage, and can't avoid turning to face them, they are already halfway out of the room.

This is my life.

My children will share a room with me for exactly as long as they have to.

My children are afraid of me.

*

The rain has gotten worse outside. I set the cup of tea down on the bedside table and I put both of my hands on the window, trying to feel it, trying to make reality feel real to me.

Funny how the weather outside knows its destiny. The storm knows what it's supposed to do. The rain, the clouds, they all form this pattern of reality. They know their purpose on Earth. Why can't I understand the meaning of my own life?

Amelia stirs a little bit, positions herself better and goes back to sleep, not even noticing that I am by the window, staring and thinking all these thoughts. I look at her and a small little smile comes over my lips. Why can't other parts of my life have the same effect, bringing the same little smile? I'm not just saying that because she's my wife or because I love her. I'm saying that because she is the most incredible person I've ever met. The man that I am, the man that exists each day is a man that she accepts completely, unconditionally, never asking questions. She just looks at me and sees a man, a good man, a wonderful man, and I think it's remarkable how she can feel that way.

What's remarkable about Amelia is that she wakes up doing this every single day. Her mindset is unbelievable, the way she judges people. Funny, I used the word "judge" but that's exactly what she doesn't do. She completely accepts everyone for what they are, how they are, and works with them. Amelia has been like that since the first day I met her.

Right at this moment, lightning spikes and thunder rolls. I look back outside at that reality. The fact that rain falls to the ground is one hundred percent true. So simple. Why can't I have that simplicity?

*

Amelia and I met in 1992 at the company we both worked for. I had been there a year and had worked my way up to supervisor. I saw her the first day she started work and immediately was attracted to her. I guess physically she caught my eye. She was a beautiful young lady, brunette, nice figure, dressed properly, sophisticated, and her clothing and hairstyle matched her personality. She called me on the phone about a problem, a situation that needed a supervisor's assistance. Immediately I noticed she had a calming, pleasant voice, willing to be helpful with her client's problems and open to suggestions, critiques and criticisms to assist her without any reluctance on her part. I was amazed how readily she accepted my suggested solution to her customer service problem. That type of personality and attitude is rare.

That was the first stirring I felt towards realizing she was a special person. I asked her at the end of the call what her horoscope sign was, and she answered Aries. The reason I say that is because that morning, reading my horoscopes for fun, never taking them seriously, I was told I would be falling in love with an Aries. I know this sounds so crazy.

We finished our workday at the same time and saw each other by the elevators when we were going home. I politely said goodnight to her, and she replied goodnight, and we went our separate ways.

A year went by with us just being work friends, talking and listening to each other but not dating. That entire year, though, I felt something for her, and I wanted to start dating, but I didn't think it was a good idea, so we just remained friends.

Two years had gone by, and I had decided to leave this company and find a new employer. Now we worked at separate companies, I finally had the guts to ask her out and she accepted. In the months that followed I got to learn more about her, seeing how well adjusted to life this young lady was by accepting things and always finding the best in anyone she met. I knew I had a rare gem, a diamond in my hands. We started dating seriously, learning more about each other, about our families, the way we think, our politics, our morals.

Everything matched perfectly between us.

Another year was up, and I knew I would not let this wonderful woman get away. I knew that she was the one to share my life, to have a family, to raise children with. It is thirty years now since we got married and I still feel that way.

It doesn't mean we didn't have our ups and downs, or difficulties, as all married couples go through. And that's normal couples. I don't know at what point she realized I would bring – let's say – something different to our own marriage. Guess I must have hid it pretty well during our courtship. Or she saw it but she thought she could cure me with love.

Make no mistake, it is her mindset that got us this far. Most of the mistakes or things that conflicted in our marriage, I have to say, were due to me. Some of it was that I was forever torn between what I knew to be true, and the expectations forced upon me by my parents and extended family. I know they meant well but they constantly caused friction in the marriage.

And then there was the other crap. Which I will come to.

But, what a remarkable person she turned out to be. We had a perfect wedding and a beautiful honeymoon in Japan and Hawaii. That year planning the wedding we bought a home. I thought my life could not get any better.

*

So here I am on a wet, miserable morning with a thunderstorm outside, safe and warm in a nice home with a wonderful wife, two beautiful children, adorable Barney, and I am miserable. How can this be, since I have everything a person wants in life?

My past controls my present and future. I don't know how

to handle this problem.

What I do know is that my pain and struggles are hurting Amelia and my kids and it's not fair on them. It's not right for them to wake up and be miserable all day long because of me. There's got to be a better way.

I walk quietly around the bed, running my fingers through my hair. I lean down and give her that soft kiss I was planning. She smiles without opening her eyes. I feel a calming hand gently reach out and take mine.

"What are you doing?"

Amelia, still under the covers and with her head on the pillow, opens her eyes and smiles at me. I see her beautiful face staring at me without judgment, noncritical, just staring at a man. Without any words between us we both know what I'm thinking. She is feeling bad for me because she knows I'm thinking the same about myself. We are so in sync.

"I'll fix breakfast and then I'll take our stuff to the laundromat," I say.

"Okay."

*

I'm up and dressed and I'm carrying the laundry basket on my hip. Like I used to carry the kids when they were little. I thump on each of their doors.

"Laundry day!"

I had breakfast in an empty kitchen, of course. They hadn't emerged again from their own rooms. Lying low, waiting for Dad to leave the house so they can leave themselves.

I know Amelia has a busy day ahead of her with her work

as a travel consultant. She's good at it, and so they keep giving her even more to do, which is fine. As if I needed any reason to be even prouder of her. We never wanted to be the kind of home where Dad goes out to work and Mom stays at home and looks after the place.

But then I retired early due to a disability, so now it's the other way round anyway. I try to help the best I can, and since our washing machine is broken, I must go down to the laundromat. I really don't mind being the one to take care of the household. Being a stay-at-home father never bothered me, nor did I feel emasculated. I just didn't like the fact that I had no choice.

And I know this sounds strange, but doing the family's laundry is therapeutic, calming. It's so strange how a normal everyday place is somewhere where I can find peace. I get the laundry all set up and sit there, listening to the humming of the washers and the dryers. I can close my eyes and rest. I feel so comfortable for that hour of time, all by myself, just thinking.

Daniel's door is first. He tips what's in his basket into mine.

"You have a great day at school," I tell him, smiling. In his room, on his own turf, his smile back at me is genuine. Daniel is something like my wife, very quiet, introverted, doesn't have a judgmental bone in his body and he always tries to accept things the way they are and not see them negatively. In fact, he makes excuses for them and tries to get along, whereas Miranda's more like me. She decides that if things are not good, they need to be fixed.

"Thanks, Dad."

Miranda is next, and if there's a smile there, it's hiding. She just holds her bag up and drops it into the basket. She always bags her dirty stuff up. I think she just feels weird at the thought of her Dad going through her underwear. I mean, I can see her point, but what does she think I do with it at the laundromat? I have to get it into the machine somehow. Out of sight, out of mind, I suppose. She's just private.

"You have a great day," I tell her too.

She tilts her head slightly. Like she's accepting a point in a debate without prejudice, not committing to anything.

"I love you, Dad."

No thanks, or anything like that. But I think she means it.

I love you. Those three words are so simple, so truthful. I know they love me. But that just makes their hurt even worse.

We had a big scene a few months back, Miranda and me. She found the courage to come and tell me how she really felt and it was a big eye opener for me. She told me that as a little girl, she never felt peace in our home and was scared every time I walked into a room. In fact she used to like going to bed early just to run away from me, because she couldn't leave the house.

I had thought she was just a well behaved child.

I was waiting for her to say, "But that was then and I'm better now..." It never came, though. This was the ongoing situation, I realized. She was just better able to cope with it as an adult.

But the fault was still mine and she still expected me to do something about it.

So that is where we are now. Stuck in mid-negotiation.

It breaks my heart that she feels this way. I don't want anyone in my family to feel like that.

I'm in the kitchen, at the door that leads into the garage. I tip the contents of the basket into the laundry bag and sling it over my shoulder, while with my spare hand I feel for my wallet and the car keys.

"I'll see you all later!" I call to the house at large. I know everyone will be gone by the time I get back.

If there are any responses, they are behind closed doors and I don't hear them.

*

I'm in the car, my white Lexus, driving through Manhasset with this big laundry bag full of dirty clothes. I time these trips for just after the work rush, so the traffic is easy.

The laundromat is one in a row of shops, which is next to the parking lot, which is next to the park. Nothing special to look at but it's special to me. The front wall is basically glass, one big window, so you can see right in. Machines to one side, table down the middle and a cubicle on the other side where the manager works.

I park the car, go in and get myself ready. I like to go during the week while the rest of the world is working. I'm usually the only person in the laundromat and for me that's just perfect. That's one of the benefits of retiring early in life. In this part of the day I feel like the whole world is going on with their lives and I'm invisible, able to hide with no one to disturb me.

I see my favorite machine available in the corner, in the back of the room on the right side, next to the door to the storeroom. I decide to use two machines. The laundry comes out better that way.

I sit down in my favorite chair and stretch my legs out, putting one ankle on top of the other. The laundromat is modern, all the machines are clean and well-ventilated. I hear them humming. The white noise is so soothing. You can find anything in white noise. You will hear a tune you had long forgotten, see a scene that has long been out of mind. Figures from the past loom out of it, coalescing before you like characters emerging from the fog. I sit back, close my eyes and I can be comfortable.

But not for long. On this occasion, all the wrong thoughts come flooding back out of the sound, vividly, right in plain sight. Woah, wrong track! My eyes fly open and I shake my head to clear them away.

I look around the room and there's absolutely no one else there except the manager of the laundromat. A nice old lady named Bertha, who says hello to me every time I walk in, her lips curling around the inevitable dangling cigarette. She lurks in her cubicle with a computer and more paperwork than you would think was possible. I mean, how many sheets of paper do you need to run a place like this? It's funny how we see each other once a week but we don't really know who we are. We just smile and say hello cordially to one another. Life goes on for both of us. What's good is that she's there if something goes wrong or if I need some extra quarters.

The sun is bright outside but I feel like I have a shadow inside me. I can't get rid of the darkness that follows me every step I take, every moment I live. The ghosts of my past life need to remain in the past, not be part of the present and especially not continue into my future. The worst part is that I think I'm getting comfortable living in misery. Accepting these feelings as part of my life, like the need for air or water. I'm secure in my unhappiness. Dealing with it would be a step into the unknown. I prefer certainty.

When you reach that comfort zone, that's when you know you have hit rock bottom.

I try again. With my earphones on, I close my eyes and listen to quiet white noise sounds. This time I deliberately send my mind down the track that should lead to good things. The last thought in my head as I fall asleep in my chair is to wonder what the white noise will send me this time.

BANG!

CHAPTER 2

Hey babe! Spare room still available? Just say if you want it. But quick. Not fair to keep others waiting. Hugs.

Miranda studied the screen in her hand. Then she let her head fall back against the rest, and closed her eyes, and groaned.

She had heard her phone ping just as she was getting into the car. She was still sitting like that now, with the door still open, one leg in the foot well, one still resting on the ground.

Two heavy thumps on the car's roof, and she convulsed. Almost dropped the phone. Heart pounding, she looked up. Daniel grinned down at her, ducking his head below the top of the door. Dark hair poking through the vents of his cyclist's helmet, eyes hidden behind the rainbow glaze of his mirror goggles, big cheesy grin his only defining feature.

"Jesus! Dan, don't do that."

"It's okay. He left five minutes ago." Daniel nodded his head over at the garage. It still stood open and there was no Lexus in it.

"I know, but..." Miranda silently cussed herself for her jumpiness. She looked at him again as he went to wheel his bike out of the garage and slam the door back down. Sleek in spandex, day clothes in the pack on his back. She laughed. "You look like Calvin's dad."

He looked over his shoulder and stuck his tongue out.

"So, wassup?"

"Oh!" She groaned again, bumped her head back against the rest, then held up the phone. "Tanya's still asking."

Tanya was her best friend outside the family. A fellow nursing student. She had an apartment share and was forever on Miranda's case, inviting her to come live with her and her room mate. It would be so *cool*. It would be so *great*.

The smile wavered. Behind the mirror goggles she imagined him looking thoughtful.

"Oh."

There was so much in that one syllable. An entire conversation's worth.

They were as close as any brother and sister could be. Daniel was only a year older. He always said he couldn't remember a time without her. A world with no Miranda.

And like all children, they took what they knew from their parents. Just accepted it as given, until time and experiences of their own let them put their own glosses on things. Apply their own interpretations and understandings.

So, they had thought life with Mom and Dad was totally normal. They knew they didn't always like it. They were often unhappy and frequently afraid. It wasn't like that on TV but right from a very young age, they knew that TV was just make believe. Out here in the real world, didn't that happen to everyone?

Then they started kindergarten. They made friends, they visited other kids' homes. They saw how other people lived.

And it turned out – no, it *didn't* happen to everyone.

Just to them.

"You know, we're both way too old to be living at home, right?"

Daniel shrugged. This was safe ground.

"We save money this way."

"It's not the only reason," she said quietly, and even behind his mirror goggles he suddenly couldn't quite meet her eyes. He covered it up by fumbling with his helmet strap, tightening it beneath his chin.

"No."

They couldn't leave home because of Mom. If they left then Mom would be on her own. With him.

"And if we're just staying for her – heck, Dan, the three of us could afford a place on our own."

"Hey," he said softly. So softly. It was understanding and rebuke and chastisement all rolled into one syllable. She had gone somewhere none of them should, and they both knew it. Even though she couldn't see his eyes, she could feel them boring into hers.

Miranda loved her brother more than life but she also *knew* him. He would always seek to understand, always take the non-confrontational way – and if that proved non-viable then sometimes, just a little, he would slide into self-deception to keep things quiet.

Whereas she held that there was nothing more sacred than truth. If that was how things were, that was how you said it. However uncomfortable it was.

It didn't help her temper that she knew exactly whose

DNA was responsible for that. Though at least she was better at self control.

She sighed.

"You know Dad and I had that talk? A while back? We... We got real close. I think. It was the closest I've ever seen him come to saying sorry out loud. I know that this... whatever it is with him, it's old and it's deep-rooted. It won't just solve itself overnight. I'm working on forgiving him and he's... Well, I *think* he's trying... So, you know, is it fair on him to move out? Am I giving him a chance?"

Daniel said nothing. They looked at each other.

"It's got to change, Dan," she whispered.

"Yeah. I know."

They stayed together for a moment longer. Silent. Not repeating the same old things over and again because they had already been said so many times. Then he slapped the roof of her car another time, and swung his leg over his bike saddle.

"So, see you later."

"Not if I see you first."

"Ha ha!" he called over his shoulder. But he was already half way down the drive and coasting out into the road. A couple of firm kicks on the pedals and he was off to work.

Miranda slipped her phone into her purse without answering the message. She slid the car into reverse, pulled back into the road and headed off in the other direction.

CHAPTER 3

I come awake with a start as the laundromat's door slams. I leap up and look around but I don't see anything. I feel a blast of air flying by me.

"This is crazy – what's going on?" I think.

A group of kids are looking through the window of the laundromat, faces up close to the glass and hands shielding their eyes. We look at each other. Whatever they're expecting, it's not me.

"Let's get out of here," I hear one of them say. I go back to my seat, still all jangled up and not knowing why. I settle back down, ready to close my eyes and try to go back to the good place again.

But there's another sound now added to the white noise of the machines. I hear someone breathing heavily, rapidly. Nothing obscene. Like a trapped animal. I follow it with my ears. Then I get up and walk slowly back to the storeroom. I push the door open slowly and see this kid.

He's sitting on a chair at the back. Feet on the seat, knees up in front of him, hands clasped together. If he's a trapped animal then he has nowhere left to run.

I ask, "Are you OK?"

But he doesn't say anything. He just looks at me.

Some people say I have no imagination but some things I can work out pretty easily.

"You can come out. Those kids are gone."

I go back to my seat without looking around. I've left the choice with him.

He follows me and sits on the next chair. He puts his backpack on the chair next to him, between us. The kid is about 5 feet 4 inches tall. His hair is parted in the middle, his face is ravaged with pimples and he has the saddest eyes I've ever seen. He must be about fourteen or fifteen years old.

"Are you OK? Do you need help? Do you need to call anyone?"

He doesn't say a word. Just stares ahead.

"Why are you running away from those kids?" I ask. He still doesn't answer me. He goes cautiously up front to look outside the window to see if they are gone. You can see he doesn't know what to do. He looks up and down, he looks outside, he looks at me. Trapped animal. I ask him to come and sit down for a minute and take a break. We sit with a chair between us, and I try to find out more.

"Those kids before, were they following you?"

He doesn't answer. He just looks at the floor. He's pretty well answered my question and now he's answering questions I haven't asked. Like, *why* were they following him? Well, there are plenty of reasons why kids run after each other. It could be a game. It could be a gang thing, one member trespassing into another's territory. I could run through all the options if I wanted.

But he and those kids outside, they look pretty much the

same. Same age, same way of dressing. They're probably his classmates.

This kid is not acting. I can see he was being bullied.

"Shall I call someone to pick you up?"

He just shakes his head to answer with a no.

"How long have those kids been picking on you?"

Now he looks to the right, away from me, and as he turns away I see tears rolling down his face. He quickly tries to wipe them away with his shirtsleeves and is hoping I didn't notice. I give him that dignity. I hear the washing machine finish its spin, so I stand up to take the clothes and put them in the dryer.

When I turn back to my chair, the kid is gone.

I look in the storage room, but he is not there. I turn around to scan the rest of the store. Not there either. No one else about, apart from Bertha up front in her office smoking, even though there are signs all over saying "No Smoking."

He's a fast mover. Maybe he needs to be. But if he's not here then at least he must have decided it was now safe to go home.

I walk back to my seat, shaking my head, putting my fingers through my hair, and I exhale a stream of angry air. Ghosts are gathering around me. The ghosts that ruined my high school years and that still ruin my life today.

Why does it have to be this way? Why do people enjoy bullying and tormenting another person? Why did a group of people get together to inflict pain on someone whose biggest crime was just existing on Earth? That boy didn't do anything to those kids. I was sure of it, just as I didn't do anything to the kids that picked on me back in my high school years.

It brings back to me a day that I will never forget. Well, there are many days I will never forget but this is one of them. When I was fifteen a group of kids decided to treat me this same way. They walked behind me, laughing, playing at tripping me up as I was trying to walk home.

There's two possible reactions to this kind of thing, two options for us to select one of. Flight, or fight. They have the same effect on us. They flood our system with adrenaline and turn up our breathing to get more oxygen into our bodies to cope with the load we are about to put on them.

It took all my guts, all my energy, but I chose fight. I turned and swung my English textbook and smashed one of the kid's faces. I hit him so hard that he lost his balance and fell to the ground, bleeding through his nose and mouth.

The other kids were in shock, for a couple of seconds, and then they all jumped on top of me. I got punched, kicked in the face, hair pulled. They did everything they could to inflict pain. These kids went nuts trying to get revenge for what I had done to their friend. Never mind that they were the ones who started bullying me and made my life miserable just for walking myself home. They all had such rage in their eyes. If they were able to kill me and get away with it, I am sure they would have tried.

I shake my head to try to get rid of the memory. I think about this kid and how his life might play out in the coming years. It was a bleak existence for me and could be for him. I know it, I remember it, all too well.

*

The dryer sounds its alarm, indicating that my clothes are

ready. I take everything out in a pile and dump it all on the table and sort it and fold it. I take a final look around to check I have everything, and then I go out.

As I am walking to my car, I hear a lot of kids laughing and screaming.

"Fuckin' faggot!"

"Piece of shit!"

How do you shout something like that and still sound like you're laughing? I look over.

They are on the edge of the parking lot, at the end of the row of shops. There's five or six of them and they are surrounding the boy I just saw in the laundromat. He is on the floor on his knees, trying to protect his face with his hands, while the rest of the kids are beating the hell out of him.

Flight or fight. Earlier he chose flight. Looks like he chose fight this time. Or maybe he stuck with flight, sensible choice, only this time they caught him.

Now, I am a grown-up. I have natural authority over a gang of kids. They don't know me but that doesn't matter. These aren't inner city gangsters hardened by a life of crime from the cradle. They are Manhasset teenagers, like my son Daniel was ten years ago. I can step right in and stop this right now.

I know exactly what to do. I get in my car and go home.

You're thinking, "Huh?"

I knew how the kid felt inside, because I've been there. I know it would kill him for me to notice and come and help him. He would rather have me leave, not see this, ignore what was happening. He would rather suffer all this mental and physical trauma than have me – have any adult – look at him with pity and sorrow. He would hate that more than he hated the kids picking on him.

I know this because that's how I felt. That's the worst part about this whole situation.

So, I turn my key and drive away, leaving the howls and screams behind me. *Their* howls and screams. *He* doesn't make a sound. I know that leaving the kid to be beaten is what he wanted me to do.

It is so sickening that the remedy was for me to walk away and not do anything. That the shame he felt hurt more than the kids abusing him.

And it lights a dark fire within me.

*

I am the first to arrive home. I put all the laundry away in its cupboards and drawers. Rather, I throw each item in and I slam the doors and drawers shut.

The day crawls on and my darkness only festers. When I go to the kitchen to start dinner, I am smashing the cabinet doors as I get the ingredients together and banging things on top of the counter.

Miranda walks in and right away I yell at her because she is in a happy mood. She stops and looks at me and I see her happiness just fade away. Her face goes blank. Then she shakes her head, goes to her room and shuts the door. Her remedy for the abusive situation that is once again my fault.

About an hour later Amelia and Daniel come home. We all sit down to have dinner together. Amelia and Daniel are quiet as usual. They are never the ones to start a conversation. Miranda is back in her happy mood, humming a song, and once again I snap at her. I tell her to stop singing. My daughter's happiness offends me.

Why? What was she doing so wrong? She was enjoying our family time together.

I sense the silence settle down over the table like a shroud. If no one talks then no one offends me.

Once I was abused and now, I have become the abuser.

*

Amelia keeps it until we are ready for bed. It's the first time we are alone together. Then she turns to me.

"You're doing it again. That attitude of yours is ruining the family."

I tell her, "Shut up. I had a bad day."

"A bad day?" she says. "What did you do? How could you have a bad day?"

What she's *saying* is, "I know your routine – in all of that, what could go wrong enough to make you act like this?" It's a simple, logical statement, trying to make sense of faulty data.

What I *hear* is, "How could *you* have a bad day?" So much packed into that "*you*". A jeering, finger pointing, sneering "*You*". How could *you* – Mr. No Job, Mr. No Prospects, Mr. Failure – how could *you* do anything to have a bad day?

I glare at her. I could kill her right at that moment. Instead I go to the bathroom and slam the door behind me.

I know I am wrong. She was just trying to help, and I made things worse. I sit on the toilet lid, my elbows on the sink, my face in my hands. And I cry uncontrollably with the same force as the thunderstorm and rain the night before.

CHAPTER 4

I slide into bed next to Amelia and once again I am just looking at her. She is sound asleep. She had a very busy day again with work, and then she came home. For most people, that's when you're meant to relax after a hard day. Not when the hard work begins.

I look over at the TV but decide to skip it. I am just not in the mood to watch anything.

It has been over forty years! Forty years since all that stuff happened to me. The same stuff that was happening to that kid today. It's still fresh. It still interferes with my life and so with the lives of my wife and children.

My life was fine up until I started freshman year in high school. I came from a good home, with all the normal pros and cons. I have three older brothers. We had a normal I love you, I hate you relationship. They spent their time looking down on me, but if we fought it was because we were each other's to fight. If someone else tried to pick on any of us, the rest would form a solid wall against them. The family stood together.

My dad was a domineering, old-fashioned-minded kind of guy. Okay, that's what I say on a good day. On a bad day I'll say he was a terrible father – but still an excellent father-in-law to my wife and even better grandfather to my children. I came to realize after far too long that he did love me – just, within his own terms of reference, he had no way of showing it. I saw this and came to love him back when I married at the age of 29. I always felt that Dad believed I became a man when I married Amelia. He never admitted to that suspicion but I think I am correct in that thinking.

And my mother was a gentle and loving soul who always tried to please her husband and children.

None of them had a clue what was happening to me every day at school and I kept it that way. I was too ashamed and embarrassed to tell any of them – until I did, and it didn't work out well, but we'll come to that later.

Amelia moves a little in our bed, making herself more comfortable without waking up. She is sound asleep. I lie back on the pillow and stare up at the ceiling. I can't fall asleep. I exhale a long sigh, eyes wide open. Those horrible memories, still so vivid and clear in my mind.

I yell inside my head, "STOP, STOP, STOP!" I rub my eyes in the hope that I will rub away the memories too. That the replays in my head will stop. I roll over, shift about, try to position my body in bed in the hope I will find a comfortable spot. Luck is on my side. I am able to clear my head, calm myself down, and fall asleep.

*

It's been a week now and life has gone on as usual in the Rato household.

I became medically retired at 53, though my first disease was diagnosed when I was nineteen years old. I have Crohn's disease. That's an immune-related condition. My gastrointestinal tract is on a constant state of high alert, ready to defend itself against... Well, anything. It doesn't even really know itself. In real-life terms it means I live with chronic inflammation, starting at my stomach and moving all the way on downwards. Plus a host of secondary conditions, just to remind me that I'm ill, should I ever need it.

It's controllable, with meds and lifestyle adjustment. I was able to lead a normal life with Crohn's – working, getting married, starting a family – until I was diagnosed with congestive heart failure.

Unlike Crohn's, the clue to that illness is in the name. My heart can't pump my blood efficiently, and that leads to build-ups of fluids in various places around my body. Again, there are meds but I have to take things easy and I do a lot of lying down. My doctors believed medical retirement would be best. I submitted the proper papers to the government and received disability.

Even though I'm disabled and even though I have to spend a lot of each day lying down, I still can do household chores. I don't mind taking care of the house, its functions and duties. I just don't like being sick and retired. But destiny always seems to take root in my life, taking control and telling me how to live it. I always must follow the path destiny bestows on me, whether I like it or not. So, I adapt and acclimate myself to make it work out.

My wife and children and I all do the usual routine as I get ready for laundry day. They always have their washing ready for me. Everyone knows I go to the laundromat this exact day and time every week, as it is empty. I like it better that way. Just me, the machines, Bertha and her cigarettes.

I collect all the usual things to take with me. Soap, laundry bag, fabric softener sheets, cell phone, wallet, and my water bottle. I get into my car and drive off.

Bertha is in her office, taking care of business while smoking her brains away. I see my machine in the back on the right-hand side, the one I like, with the chair next to it, and I get myself ready and all set up. I load the laundry, sit down and wait for the machine to go on. I look all around. There's nobody in this place. It is like the world ended and I'm the only one left with Bertha on Earth.

As usual the humming sound of the washing machine is soothing. It's relaxing and makes me feel calm. I close my eyes, stretch my legs forward and rest.

I'm aware of someone sitting down next to me. I open my eyes and see Bertha, peering at me with concern. I might recoil a little. Not because I don't like her, just out of surprise at the proximity.

"How are you feeling?"

I tell her I'm fine. Though it might sound more like a question: "I'm... fine?" She looks worried, like something is wrong with me. I tell her again I feel fine, maybe with a bit more conviction, and thank her for her concern. She pats my knee and walks back to her office.

I stare at her back while she sits down at her computer, and I think to myself, "What the hell was that all about?" She doesn't notice that I am looking at her.

That was weird. She never did that before, never came up

to me and asked how I felt, never showed any type of concern except for my being a customer.

But I'm not getting any answers so I close my eyes again and go back into my comfort zone, listening to the humming of the washing machine, letting the white noise wash over me.

*

Bang! My eyes fly open. Someone has slammed the door of a washing machine on their own laundry load.

It is that kid, that kid I saw the other day. The one that was running away, the kid that got a good ass kicking. The one I helped by not helping.

We look at each other. He puts the soap in his machine and presses the start button. I hear the beeping as the program begins and the whir of the pumps as it clears away any water from the last wash, before starting afresh with the new one. Then he comes and sits down, next to me but a chair away, like last time.

Different clothes, same uniform. T-shirt and jeans. They look clean, so someone is taking care of him. I know what the kicking he got would have done to what he was wearing. What did his parents say to that?

Hairstyle is the same, and when he glances sideways at me, it's just long enough to get a glimpse of those eyes again. Deep enough to hold all the sorrow in the world.

Bertha is watching us but not saying anything. I ask the kid how he is feeling. Once again he doesn't answer me. He just looks forward, straight ahead.

"Are you OK?"

He still doesn't answer my question so I leave him alone. I close my eyes, rest my head back and try to take a nap. Suddenly, I hear in a low voice, "I-I-I-I'm doing OK."

I open my eyes and turn to him.

"I'm glad to hear that. I saw what happened to you last week."

I guess that was the wrong thing to say because he gets up quickly and is walking fast to leave.

"Wait! I'm sorry, please don't go." He stops dead in his tracks.

Why am I so concerned? Because I know how terribly lonely he must be. I will spare his pride and not interfere with his abuse, but I cannot let him be lonely.

"Please, come back and sit down."

He turns slowly and comes back to his chair.

"What's your name?" No answer. So, I go first. "Hmm, um, well, my name is Mr. Rato. What's yours?"

Still no answer. He really is locked up. I know I have to really go slow. I have to pick my way past a lot of barriers.

My washer makes the finishing noise. I get up to put things in the dryer. When I get back to my seat to fetch a fabric softener sheet, it sounds like he murmurs a name. I don't catch it.

"I'm sorry, what was that?"

He speaks a little louder, maybe not normal volume but I hear him this time.

"Your name is Nicholas?"

He says it again at a normal level.

"Nicholas? Your name is Nicholas?" He nods. I say, "Well,

nice to meet you, Nicholas." Then I say again, "I'm Mr. Rato." We're not really at the stage where an adult gives a kid his first name.

He looks down and I hear him say, "Hello, Mr. Rato."

I ask him, "So, no school today?" No answer. I decide to keep talking. "It's OK. Are you feeling sick? You're not feeling well? Are you tired?"

It is like getting blood from a stone. Eventually he says, "I'm not feeling well so I stayed home from school. My parents don't know."

I think of my son, the teacher. I answer, "Well, do you think that's a good idea?" He looks down. I say, "Look, I won't say anything, it's OK, you need a day off sometimes, I understand."

Daniel would not, but he needn't know.

"Thanks," he says. Small smile. It only makes his mouth twitch. Doesn't do much for the rest of his face and it will take a lot of smiling to erase the sorrow from those eyes. But it's a start. I try to keep the conversation going.

"So, where are you from? Do you live near?"

He answers, "Not far."

I continue. "Doing laundry for your family?"

I guess that too was a wrong question because he gets all nervous. His eyes dart from side to side and he shifts about like there's ants in his pants.

He says, "I wanted to do my own laundry. I-I-I-I didn't want my parents to see my clothes."

"Why not?" I ask, and he shrugs his shoulders in an "I-don't-know" way.

I notice there's a light gold chain around his neck. A small cross is hanging on it. I could ask him about that, to make conversation, but maybe I've asked enough questions.

I can't tell him I know about him being bullied. He knows I know, so what good would it do? So I take that bit as read and go straight to the next bit.

I tell him, "Nicholas, look, let's agree you can say anything you want. I promise you this, it will always be between us. Don't ever feel like I'm going to call your parents or your school, OK?"

He says, "OK."

We talk some more. He tells me his age, which is fourteen. What school he is going to (not the same one Daniel and Miranda were at, or where Daniel now works). All that kind of stuff – safe, easy questions that I know won't close him up again. I can see he is starting to feel comfortable with me, like he has begun trusting me more and more. We talk until his clothes are done. He gets up and collects his stuff and stuffs it into his bag.

I ask, "Don't you want to use the dryer?"

He shakes his head. "No."

I tell him, "Look, Nicholas I'm always here, this same day, same time, every week, so if you ever just want to visit and hang out, talk, I'm here, OK?" He nods yes. At that moment the dryer buzzes to indicate that it is done. I get up to collect my family's clothing, and I gather up all my belongings that I brought with me. I look around to say goodbye to Nicholas, but he is gone. I look all around the laundromat but he is nowhere to be found.

Passing by Bertha's office I call, "See you next week, take

care."

She answers, "You too," and breathes out a cloud of cigarette smoke. I just smile to myself and walk outside.

I look right and I look left – no one in sight.

"How does he come and go so quickly?" I think. I walk to my car and go home.

For the rest of the day I think about this kid Nicholas and his deep, so-sad eyes.

Did I ever look like that? I thought I hid it so well. My family never suspected.

Did I ever meet their eyes long enough for them to notice?

Five or six times as I go through the day, I realize I've stopped doing whatever I was at – some small, mundane task – because instead I'm thinking about Nicholas. Each time I shake my head, just thinking how much alike we are, this kid and myself.

But then I am thinking about the kids and Amelia coming home. I need to get dinner started and take care of the rest of the night.

*

We get through this meal time, all being our normal selves. Amelia and Daniel quiet or giving one-word answers to all my questions, and Miranda being her jovial self, happy and just not able to keep quiet. Normal family routine.

Maybe they think I've had a good day. They wouldn't understand if I told them it was just the opposite. I'm still so distracted by Nicholas that I can't really join in with what they're saying. Which means I don't get upset by it. So that's a win, for them, in a weird kind of way.

Later, Amelia and I get ready for bed. I am lying down on my side. Amelia gets into bed, kissing my shoulder, saying goodnight.

"I'm dead tired today. My phone was nonstop with eight calls on hold all day waiting. I'm beat."

"OK, darling, get some sleep. Goodnight," I say. I blow a kiss at her. She is sleeping as soon as her head hits the pillow.

I look straight ahead, eyes adjusting to the dim light that makes it through the drapes. The lamp, the night table, the entrance to our walk-in closet are all outlines right in front of my eyes, but I don't see them. I see the laundromat, the machines, Bertha and Nicholas. It is all so vivid in my mind still. Especially the kid and his sad, lonely eyes.

If his eyes could talk, I have a bad feeling about the horrible stories they would scream out at me.

And because I've been there, I know I need to do something. Just being there at the laundromat isn't enough.

The problem is, I don't know what else I can do.

CHAPTER 5

*T*om *Cruise…*, Amelia thought vaguely as the seventh red light lit up on her phone and the client on line number one kept chatting into her ear and the busyness of the office swam around her.

"That's correct, Mrs. Adams." She spoke into the headset while her fingers tapped at the keys and her eyes darted over the information on the screen in front of her. Mrs. Maureen Adams. Resident, Manhasset. Age 72… Okay. "Any airport scanner will let you show your screen with the boarding pass on it…"

What was that Tom Cruise movie?

The querulous voice spoke in her ear.

He was… Oh, yes, he was an agent, a sports agent, trying to hustle for business. His phone was all lit up as clients waited on hold…

"You don't have a smartphone. Well, that is fine too. You can print the email off when you receive it, and it will include the boarding code…"

And he was talking to this one pain-in-the-ass client who would not let him go…

"You won't have a printer where you're going. Not a problem, Mrs. Adams, just go to the airport check-in desk on arrival and they will print the boarding passes off…"

And one by one the lights were going out as the other guys took the calls until it was just the pain-in-the-ass client left…

"You're very welcome, Mrs Adams. Have a great flight."

Oh look, another light has come on.

"Good afternoon, Traveltime, thank you for holding, I'm Amelia Rato, how may I assist you?"

What was that movie?

"That is correct, ma'am – and yes, we might have just the thing for you. Seven days in London…?"

Traveltime had grown to three branches in the time that Amelia worked there, but she was still at branch number one, the original. Four rows of desks in front of a plate glass window. The front two rows with flesh and blood customers sitting at each of them, talking to advisors, while more walk-in customers waited in the seats behind them, talking to each other or on their own phones. The back two rows had Amelia and her colleagues, dealing with phone calls. Tim, founder and CEO, made sure they rotated so no one got stuck with just one job.

I wish some of these lights would go out…

"I will just check that... Yes, we could certainly arrange an onward flight from London Heathrow to Paris Charles de Gaulle…"

Oh, yes! Jerry Maguire! We saw it when it came out, my husband and me. We'd been married for about a year, no kids then…

Traveltime specialized in off-season vacations. Packages for when the schools had gone back and the resorts were emptier, and cheaper.

What that meant was the clientele were typically at the older end of the age spectrum. And that very often meant a greater degree of hand-holding for the clients.

Which Amelia was absolutely fine with. They were people who had lived a life and given their time and energy to make the world she had grown up in. It was a pleasure and a privilege to help them in return. They had earned their way to where they were now and why shouldn't they take the me-time they were entitled to?

And she always felt a greater connection when you were talking, rather than just doing it online. There was always something new to learn from them, something to share. A mutual respect, a bit of give and take on either side.

"You're welcome... Yes, I quite understand, if I can..."

Click.

"Well, goodbye then..." Amelia murmured.

Sometimes the client hadn't got the memo. Sometimes it was more take than give.

Amelia paused, took a couple of breaths, reached out to press the button by the red light.

"Amelia?"

She looked up. Tim was poised, half in and half out of his office.

"Mind if I borrow you a moment? Desirée can handle the calls, right?"

Amelia glanced wryly at Desirée at the next desk; Desirée rolled her eyes but smiled and nodded. Tim had already withdrawn into his office and left the door open. Amelia got up and went in.

Tim was back behind his desk, reclining comfortably in his chair, hands folded over what was turning into a successful businessman's stomach. He was in his late thirties, hair still dark but prematurely receding.

"Take a seat!" He smiled and indicated the chair opposite with a wave. Amelia perched herself down and waited expectantly.

"Bad news!" he announced. Still smiling. He waited for her to give the puzzled frown he was obviously expecting. "For everyone else! But great for you. How do you fancy a trip to Cancún?"

It took a moment to sink in.

"Cancún, as in, Mexico?" she asked, just to make sure.

"No, Cancún, Oklahoma," he said, straight faced. Another smile. "Yes, Amelia, Mexico."

Amelia thought ahead quickly.

"The conference?"

"The conference," he confirmed. "I'm up to my neck with getting the next branch open, plus it's around Peg's due date, but I have to send someone and who better than my top advisor? Plus you'll be going with Suzanne."

His smile, she realized, was completely genuine.

Which just made her return smile feel even more fake. She could feel the tension in her face and eyes, the muscles working at pulling them into the right shape.

"That's... great."

And it was. Cancún. Responsibility and challenge. And Suzanne, her best friend from work who she hadn't seen for ages – not since she went off to head up the second office.

Tim sat up straighter in his seat, giving her a sideways frown that was slightly puzzled, slightly worried.

"Hey, you don't need to look delighted if you don't want to."

"No – sorry – thanks, Tim. That's great news and really kind of you."

"Thank *you*, Amelia. You're the one doing the hard work. I just sit back here in my room and count the money you're making me." Another sideways look. "Is there any good reason I *shouldn't* give you this?"

Suddenly Amelia could think of one hundred and one reasons not to take the offer. But then she knew that the first hundred were just small things, excuses for the massive, great big hundred and first that hung over everything.

A reason she could never share with Tim or with anyone.

"Not a single one," she said, and now she could smile genuinely because she knew it was true. There was no good reason, and he had made her the offer because she was damn good at what she did and nothing and no one could take that away from her. "Thanks, Tim. I'll let my husband know."

"You do that." Another bright smile. "He'll be delighted for you."

*

Amelia had to go to the ladies' rest room to make the call. She couldn't risk witnesses. She propped herself against the row of basins and made the call.

Be-ee-p… be-ee-ep…

Her heart hammered against her ribs in time with the ringing in her ear.

Come on, honey, pick up…

She wanted him to answer because she wanted it to be over. And she dreaded it at the same time, for the same reason.

A click and a whir as the call connected.

"Hi, honey?" He sounded pleased, a bit surprised. And slightly woozy. He had probably been lying down. She hoped he had had his phone by him. Not had to get up off the bed.

"Hi honey, say I've got news..."

Amelia realized she was gabbling. She made herself pause. Take a breath. Speak in a more measured way. Like normal people. And that was how she briefly outlined her conversation with Tim.

She came to the end very quickly, because there was not that much to say. Then she waited. The phone was slick in her hand, the sweat lubricating the plastic case.

She tried not to imagine that the silence at the other end was a gaping void.

"Mexico?" The word was quiet, neutral. Could mean anything. And then: *"Oh, sweetie, that is such great news. Well done! You so deserve it..."*

Amelia missed the rest of what he said, drowned out by the gush of relief, the roaring of blood in her ears. She tilted her head back and closed her eyes and let him carry on speaking.

The phone almost slipped from her hand and she had to grab it. As she put it back to her ear, she realized he had stopped speaking. Her turn.

"So – uh – yes, honey, I just wanted to let you know. I guess I'd better get to work before Tim changes his mind!"

"No problem, sweetheart. I'm so proud of you. See you later!"

A click, and the line went dead. Amelia closed her eyes

again and listened to her heart slowing down.

And why shouldn't he be pleased? Why shouldn't he be proud of her? He genuinely and sincerely loved her, and what husband who felt like he did would feel any other way about his wife's success?

But the fact was, she thought, as she took hold of the door handle, you just never knew.

By the time she had pulled the door open, her face was set and cheerful again and no one would ever guess that she had just avoided another mine in the eternal minefield that was her life, and her marriage.

CHAPTER 6

Amelia and I are walking in the park right next to our home. That is her favorite pastime, and since I have been sick and receiving SSI Disability, the doctors want me to walk at least half an hour a day. Daniel and Miranda are doing their own thing at home. So, we decide to go out and have a nice walk with Barney.

I love this time of year, leaving the summer and entering the fall. We have those crisp, blue-sky days where all you need is a light jacket and someone you love right next to you.

It's thirty years that I've been married to Amelia. I still like just walking and holding her hand. I always reach for her hand to hold no matter what the situation. It gives me so much pride to hold it and walk by her side. I can't explain what I feel. Just holding her hand, just having those five fingers in mine, is like finding a buried treasure full of everything you possibly could want in life. Even after thirty years of marriage I still thank God every day that she is my wife. If I should lose everything else and only have her hand to hold, I would still be the happiest man on Earth.

I turn to look at Amelia.

"Honey, it's a beautiful day, isn't it? I love these days right before the bitter winter."

"Me too," Amelia says, and leans her head on my right arm while we walk.

"So, how did your day go? Apart from the good news."

"The same as always, eight calls on hold. I never feel like I have enough time in a day to finish my workload."

I know she loves her job even though she sometimes complains about it.

I tell her, "I miss being a part of the working environment. There's something about mixing with other people, moving around, sharing ideas... This forced medical retirement wasn't my idea."

She gives my arm a squeeze.

"I know it wasn't."

"But that's destiny, so I must deal with it."

We give each other a simple smile and continue our walk.

"So, are you excited about this Mexico trip?"

She squeezes my hand harder and leans more into my right arm. As I look down, I see a big smile on her face. It's all the answer I need. I know her company only gives these business trips for merit. So, her going to Cancún is because she did extremely well this year. I'm very proud of her. Plus, she's staying at a five-star resort, in an oceanfront room, and she's going with one of her best friends from work. She deserves all this happiness. I kiss the top of her head and we continue to walk.

After a while, I say, "I can't believe the holidays are just around the corner. Thanksgiving, Christmas, and New Year's are almost on us. It's like the whole year just flew by."

"I know what you mean. The years go by faster and we get

older faster." We both chuckle and hold more tightly to each other. Loving every minute and moment together.

*

Amelia notices the time.

"The kids should be getting hungry, so I better get home and start on dinner."

"You go ahead. Barney and I want to sit a moment in the park."

She gives me her smile, lets go of my arm and heads back to our home.

I watch her walk away as I sit on a park bench in my signature style, meaning my long legs stretched out in front, my arms crisscrossed. The air, the light, the great feeling of being alive hit me. I just want to savor it a little more. I blow into my cupped hands because it is starting to get more than crisp outside, it is starting to get outright cold. I rub my hands and sit back. I put my face up with my eyes closed and feel the sun on my face. The perfect spot of cold and cloudless sunshine. I am feeling great. Great to be alive. I am looking forward to a pleasant night with my family.

I look down at Barney and say, "Well, want to go home?" He starts to run towards the house. He is freezing and wants to go home. I just laugh, thinking how cute Barney can be sometimes.

*

Amelia is getting supper ready in the kitchen, and the kids are in their rooms. I ask her if she needs help.

"No, I like having these small opportunities to cook dinner for my family."

I grab a carrot out of her hands as she tries to make a salad. She says, "Heyyyyy!" Smiling. I smile back and walk away.

"Call me when you're done," I say over my shoulder, and I take a large, crunchy bite. Then I go to watch TV, the evening news.

We all eat dinner, talk about our day. The usual happenings. Miranda and I tow the conversation along with our gift of the gab while Amelia and Daniel give their one-liners. It is a pleasant evening.

I remind everyone, "Hey guys, don't forget..." and Amelia, Daniel and Miranda all join together in unison: "Make sure I have all your laundry, I'm going tomorrow."

I start to say more but they are in unison again:

"Make sure you look everywhere so I don't miss a piece that needs cleaning!"

Miranda says, "Come on, Dad, when are you going to get a new washer?"

I draw in a breath and they all say in unison: "I'll order one this weekend."

I let the breath out.

Daniel jokes, "I think he has a thing for Bertha." I stare at them.

"Are you kidding? Wow, that's got to be some picture, guys! She is old enough to be *my grandmother*. Let alone your great grandmother. Just leave your stuff, please, thanks, guys."

Yes, it's a good night. When we turn in, my head hits the pillow and I fall right to sleep.

*

"Hi, Bertha, how's it going? Did you have a great week?"

Bertha is in her office. She waves with one hand and smokes her cigarette with the other, but she doesn't take her attention off the computer screen. I go right to the machine that I like, in the back, right-hand side. My special chair is waiting for me and as usual nobody else is around.

I load up – dirty laundry, check; soap in slot, check; door slammed shut; check. I press the buttons. Nothing. Stand back, study the machine up and down, scanning it like I can shock it into action.

"Hey, Bertha, the machine isn't working!"

This time she answers.

"You stupid ass, I told you when that happens, press the button on the right-hand side, bottom of the machine. Now stop bothering me, I got a lot of things to do."

The moment she starts talking, I remember. For some reason there's a hole in my memory and this bit of information must be exactly the right size and shape to fall right through it.

I shake my head with a smile thinking, "That lovable Bertha!"

The washers are all set up and I hear the water pouring into the machine. I make myself comfortable in my favorite chair, in my favorite position.

The washing machine starts its humming noise. The white noise always soothes me. The washer is almost at the last cycle when I hear a low voice.

"Hey, Mister. You dropped your water bottle on the floor."

My eyes open. Nicholas is in his usual place, a chair between us. I reach down and pick the bottle up.

"Thank you," I say, looking up at him. "How have you been?"

Once again, he is not much of a talker. He looks everywhere except into my eyes.

I ask him again, "How are you?"

Like they've got a life of their own, his fingers brush the neckline of his t-shirt. His neck is bare. My eyes narrow and I get a bad feeling.

"Nicholas, the last time I saw you I was admiring this little cross you have. On a gold chain. It looked like Italian gold, eighteen karats. Did you leave it at home?"

"No," he answers loudly. No one ever taught this kid to lie. He does it really badly. There is silence between us. I don't know what to do to get this kid to open and talk to me.

From Bertha's office, I hear, "What the hell is going on back there?"

I answer, "Nothing, I'm just talking to my friend here."

I see her give me a strange look over her shoulder, like one of us is mad. She shakes her head and goes back to smoking a cigarette and taking care of the bills on her desk.

"Don't mind her, kid," I tell Nicholas, "she's a nice lady, just a blabbermouth. She's a nosy, busybody person but she's got a great heart." I kind of laugh but he doesn't say anything.

I try again.

"Nicholas, what happened to your gold chain?"

"I lost it."

The lying does not improve with practice.

"You lost it, just like that?" I give him a long look, then I say, "Kid, look, I'm here to be your friend. I'm here for you to talk to. I'm here to help you with this. Do you want to tell me what happened?"

He gets up, walks to the machine and starts to talk, not looking at me.

"Wait, Nicholas, I can't hear you." Reaching out, but not touching him. "Can you turn around?"

He turns, leans back against the machine. Starts to talk to me.

"I was at school. I needed to go to the men's room."

He says it like he's answered my question in full.

"Go on?"

A pause.

"There was someone coming in behind me. There always is, isn't there? It's not unusual."

"No, it is not."

He stares straight ahead, hands hanging at his side, almost standing at attention, reciting details he has memorized. Just the facts, no inflection or tone.

"And they pushed me into one of the stalls, and they got me into a headlock, and they ripped the chain off, then they ran out of the bathroom."

He comes down out of attention and looks at me.

"But I still had to use the bathroom, so I went, and then I washed my hands and went back to class."

I am quiet for a moment. It's still sinking in.

"... Wow."

I shake my head, trying to get my brain around this. Somehow, I just know that once I have it all on board, I am not going to react well. For now there's a period of grace and I can talk rationally. "I can't believe that someone just mugged you at school. Did you report this to anyone?"

"No," he says loudly. For the first time I hear some volume in his voice.

I ask, "Did you tell your parents?"

He answers sharply, "No!"

I tell him, "Nicholas, you *must* tell your parents. They need to be told what happened, plus go down to report the mugging to your principal."

He answers, "*No!*" in a very loud voice. "I don't want to speak to anybody about this and if you tell anyone I promise you I'll never come back and speak with you again!"

This is the one thing I do know and I say it again, while I can still follow a thought and make sense.

"Nicholas, you've got to report this mugging."

He yells, "Leave me alone!" and runs out. My eyes follow him out the front door.

I hear Bertha yell at me across the room.

"Stop making all that noise out there! I can't concentrate."

Just at that point the washing machine stops, and inside my head is crashing. At least I have some routine to help me get moving again. I load the dryer, push the button to start, and sit back in my chair. I run my fingers through my hair. So many thoughts run through my mind. I picture the scene over and over. Nicholas walking into the men's room. The kid right behind him. (It must be another kid. An adult would use the staff washroom.) Pushing him through the door, dragging him into the stalls. The headlock and ripping the chain from his neck. It replays again and again. I just don't understand how we all exist in this world together and yet act this way towards each other. I just don't understand mankind anymore.

Suddenly, I hear the voice of doom. Bertha.

"Are you finished back there?"

I answer, "Yes, I'm getting my stuff and leaving."

"Good, I need peace and quiet. You make a lot of noise."

*

Nicholas is in my head all the way home and my anger is growing as I put the laundry away.

A noise like a gunshot echoes around the kitchen and snaps something in me. I wheel around and scream at a distance of a few inches into the newcomer's face.

"Do you have to make all that noise? Can't you come in the house like a civilized human being? Why are you sneaking behind me like that?"

Daniel recoils and stares in shock.

CHAPTER 7

"**O**kay, guys, let's go!"

Daniel switched on the confidence as he stepped out into the school gym, and then he saw who was in his class. No one watching would have guessed that confidence immediately got a dent knocked in it.

"Let's go!" he shouted again over the sound of laughing, chatting eighth graders. He punctuated the order with two rapid bounces of the basketball in his hands, one-two, with a sound that bounced off the walls. Gyms were good for echoes. The group of boys and girls gathered around in their gym kit, some still chatting until another couple of bounces got their attention.

Daniel had always been good at basketball, and he had found early on that the bounces were an easy way of getting the kids in line. They thought he was ancient – all of ten years older than them – but it was a skill that translated across the generations. The sporty ones paid attention because they wanted to see how he did it, and their silence made space for the less sporty ones to listen to what he was saying.

And one of the gathering crowd was Tina. She already looked worried, hanging back a little until peer pressure made her step forward and join her friends.

He casually played with the ball while he spoke, twirling it around his fingers, moving it fluidly from one hand to the other.

"So, what we're doing today is the vaulting horse..."

He led them over to the horse, feeling a bit like the Pied Piper at the head of a column of children.

The first time he had done this, he had been shadowing Mr. Sullivan, who was head of PE. He had been so relieved that he clearly had the friendliest, most co-operative group of kids ever in his class. They were putty in Mr. Sullivan's hands. They liked the older teacher and they respected him, and they did whatever he asked.

Then he had been left to handle the class on his own. Same names, same faces, totally different group. No respect for him at all. That was the closest Daniel had ever come to giving up.

In his first coffee break, over a steaming cup, Mr. Sullivan had explained the problem.

"Dan, think back to when you were at the age. What made it work for you?"

So he had taken a while to think about it, and how he had been as a kid, and it came to him. They didn't know Daniel well enough to respect him, or even like him. And they wouldn't like him until they respected him, and they wouldn't respect him until he gave them a reason to.

He had learned. Quickly. Because he had to. Mr. Sullivan had filled in the gaps for him but after that chat, it was pretty much already laid out in his head.

First, be real. Don't try to be what you're obviously not, because you will fail. They will detect the inauthentic and they will never respect it. So, don't try to be young like them. Be *you*.

But at the same time, be all things to all people. To the bros, be a bro. To the geeks, be a geek. Don't act shocked when they try to shock. If they show they know a new rude word, show that you know another ten.

Have cast iron boundaries and no favorites. Let anyone get as close to the line as they like, but if they cross it, you come down, hard. Be justice, personified.

Exalt the meek and the humble, bring down the proud. But do it gently. Not in a way that humiliates them, just a way that makes it clear you are in charge, and if there is a clash of wills then you will win.

Above all, *like* them. Enjoy their presence, because they really are a great set of kids and they deserve to be liked.

The moment that he had known would come, came.

"Coach Dan, do we have to?" Tina asked in a quiet voice. She was a kind, gentle girl, medium build, not too light or too heavy. She was popular, she had friends, no one picked on her, and she had zero self-confidence.

So he gave her his most encouraging smile.

"Tina, I really believe you can do this."

"Yeah, but you're paid to believe that, Coach!" That was one of the boys.

He couldn't deny it, but he wasn't going to engage with the argument brigade.

"Well, back in the time of the dinosaurs, and remember we're talking three presidential administrations, I couldn't do it either," he said. "Okay, guys, listen up. Here's how you *don't* do it."

The kids stood in a circle around the horse. Daniel chucked the basketball to a boy he knew could catch it without fumbling, and walked back a few yards. Then he turned to face the horse.

"You see it there, so you run up to it."

He deliberately hammed the run-up, sliding his feet back with every step that he took forward, windmilling his arms.

"It's in front of you and it looks massive!"

He ignored the kid who laughed, "That's what she said!"

"And so you let yourself falter. You're building up momentum and..." He stopped just short of the horse. "It's gone! And *then* you decide to jump." He rested both hands on the horse and swung himself up, landing on his front on the top of it with a thud. The kids laughed again. Even Tina was smiling at the clown display.

"So, here's what you *do* do. It's all one movement. The run-up, the hoist up with your arms, the vaulting over. It's not your legs that get you over the top. Your legs have done their bit by the time you reach it. What counts is the momentum you've gained. You've done kinetic energy in science, right? So, like this..."

He had their attention fixed on him as he walked back, turned, ran forward, hands on top of the horse and he vaulted effortlessly over.

"Okay guys, let's see how you do. Line up, one at a time, when you're over then circle round and we'll all have a second go..."

Most of them made it over, first time. A couple grounded themselves on top of the horse.

As soon as Tina began her run-up, Daniel knew she was

going to do what he had said not to. She was going to stop, and then jump.

She barely got off the ground. She sort of flopped herself onto the horse, then slid back to the ground. She stood at the end of the horse and looked at it sadly.

"Okay, Tina, next time," Daniel said softly. There were still other kids to come. She nodded grimly and went to rejoin the line.

"Come on, Tina!"

Daniel's head whipped up and he groaned inside. Tina's dad was up on the gallery, watching.

Normally, PE class would not be open to spectators. But Tina's dad was on the staff, and he was senior to a trainee like Daniel.

"Just do it! It's easy!"

Daniel could handle a group of kids. Handling a bad attitude adult was still beyond his skill set. He tuned the interruption out.

"Okay, guys, second time around, let's go. Remember what I said. It's all one movement. Just keep going. You'll feel light as a feather. Off you go..."

Daniel kept one eye on Tina as she watched even the kids who had grounded the first time make it over. She was biting her lip. Apart from that, it was impossible to say what she was thinking.

She started to run, hesitantly, then with more confidence, getting into her stride. Daniel let himself hope.

"Go girl!" Tina's dad was still up on the gallery, still watching. "That's it! One, two, one, two and... *ga-aah!*"

Tina's confidence had evaporated under the commentary. She did worse than last time. She just stopped, didn't even try to jump, and Daniel saw the tears in her eyes.

"Okay, Tina... want to sit this out?" he asked gently. He hated sending kids over to the side, it felt like a personal failure on his part, but there was no point just flogging them. She nodded mutely.

He glanced up at the gallery. Her dad had disappeared. That was a blessing at least.

"Well, then..."

The doors flew open as her dad came striding in. "Tina!"

Daniel saw red. It didn't matter how senior Tina's dad was. This was unacceptable. He hated ever getting into a fight but on this occasion it looked like he might have to. He squared himself up and stood in front of the approaching man.

"Sir, listen..."

The man ignored him, walked straight past and... knelt down by his trembling, quivering daughter so that their faces were on a level. Daniel watched in disbelief as he put gentle hands on her shoulders.

"Honey? I'm sorry. Sometimes I care just a bit too much. I get carried away. Look, I heard Coach Dan's advice and it was good stuff. You pay attention to what he says and you'll do fine. And me – I'll just get out of your way. You can tell me about it later, right?"

All Daniel's prepared words disappeared out of his head. He had been braced for a complete asshole of a dad and suddenly there was just this love and understanding between them. And her dad was apologizing.

The other man stood up and turned to go.

"Close your mouth, Dan, you'll catch a fly," he murmured as he walked past.

In a fairy tale, Tina would have made it over the horse the next time she tried. She didn't, but she followed Daniel's advice and she got halfway before she grounded.

The time after that, her fourth time, she jumped clear over it, and when she landed the other kids cheered and gathered around her, while she beamed as if the sun was shining just for her.

*

Daniel's mind was still whirling as he unlocked his bike and pulled it back from the stand.

"Good afternoon, Coach Dan!"

A woman's voice, gentle and kind, whose owner could usually cheer him up. He glanced over. Rosie Kendall, geography teacher, fellow bicyclist enthusiast and at one time they had been sort of getting close...

Until he had realized that he could never, ever take her home. She had found herself friend-zoned, and assumed it was her rather than him, she just wasn't his kind, and that was fine.

"Hi, Miss Kendall," he grunted. She half-paused, somehow guessed this wasn't the time for talk.

"Well, see you tomorrow!"

They mounted their bikes and kicked off in opposite directions.

*

Later, Daniel would blame it on the distraction. What he had seen. Those few moments between father and child, were just not what life had taught him. The memory stayed with him all the way as he waved his way on autopilot through the afternoon traffic. He was still processing it as he wheeled up the driveway and braked in front of the garage.

He put his bike away and pushed open the connecting door into the kitchen. He let it swing shut behind him with a bang.

And that was when he saw his father, standing with his back to him, tensed up, which should have sounded a warning bell. But it was already too late.

He opened his mouth for a friendly, "Hey, Dad," but his dad was already swinging around on him. His face was red and flecks of spittle marked the corners of his mouth.

"Do you have to make all that noise? Can't you come in the house like a civilized human being? Why are you sneaking behind me like that?"

*

"What are you talking about, Dad? I'm not even near you."

Our eyes lock and I see the shutters come down behind his. Feelings and emotions carefully blanked off so that I can't hurt him any further than I already have. Daniel makes the first move to retreat.

"I'll be in my room, Dad, if you need anything." I hear his door close slowly, softly.

I go to the sink and slam my fists on the counter. I know I'm wrong treating him that way, taking my anger out on him. I wash my hands and try to wash my face in the kitchen sink.

My eyes are full of tears and my cheeks are red. I take a deep breath, open the refrigerator and drink some cold water. I slam the refrigerator door and then lean against the counter with my hands.

The phone rings. I see that it is Amelia calling me. I hear her voice.

"*Hi, honey, you're on speaker. Miranda and I are together. We're just picking up a few things and will be home in about an hour.*"

I yell back.

"You're picking up a few things? You're just picking up a few things?" At this point I'm screaming. "Just picking up a few things, what the hell for, why are you going out? We don't need anything, we don't need you to buy anything, we don't need you to grab anything."

I hear Miranda. "*Oh shit, Mom, he's in one of those moods again.*"

I address her comment. "I'm in one of those moods? My moods are a thing? You guys are grabbing things and you're yelling at me, there's nothing for you to grab, why can't you just come home? Why do you need to go grab things in the store?"

There is a dead silence. It is only five seconds long but Amelia, Miranda and I all feel like it's a lifetime.

Amelia says, softly, "*Honey, we'll be home soon.*"

I look up to the ceiling with the phone at my ear but no words come out of my mouth. I hear Amelia say, "*Honey, you there?*"

"Yes, I'm here. Do what you need to do and just come home."

I hang up on them. I walk around the kitchen. I walk around the house. I can only imagine what Amelia and Miranda are talking about right now. I know Miranda is very upset and she's probably telling her mother she can't take it anymore and I bet Amelia is taking a deep sigh, trying to calm her down.

I go to Daniel's bedroom, knock on the door and tell him through the wood, "Daniel, I'm going out. I'll be back later. You guys eat dinner, don't wait for me."

I grab my jacket, the bigger one since it's going to be cold tonight. I grab my keys and cell phone. I lock the door and walk out, not looking back.

CHAPTER 8

6:44 p.m. The last digit on the wall clock blurred, changed. 6:45 p.m.

Amelia sat at the kitchen table, hands resting on the table top, an empty chair facing her. Daniel sat to her left and Miranda to her right. They silently met her gaze. Even Daniel's usual cheerful optimism had been replaced by something more blank, resigned, *here we go again*. Miranda's lips were twisted as though she was about to utter some word that it would not be good to say out loud, but it remained unsaid.

Every syllable of her children's body language screamed that they would rather be somewhere else, but they stayed. They were here because she and her husband had raised a pair of adults who weren't afraid to take on adult responsibility, to push through pain barriers. And that meant standing together as a threesome and facing their father as one.

She smiled at the children, her usual smile, her reassuring smile that her husband said could calm down even a wild dog. But she knew all too well that this wild dog, their father, was out there somewhere and without her guidance she knew he could get lost.

She had known this from Day One of their relationship. Just by being there, she was the one who brought him home.

His lifeline. He would reel in on that line and always come back.

It was not a role she had welcomed, once she fully understood it – a painful learning curve – but she had taken it on when she said "I do" to all those vows. She had resigned herself to it and now she accepted it with all her heart.

She looked up again at the clock. 6:49 p.m.

*

7:39 p.m. The kitchen had been cleaned. She dried her hands with the kitchen towel and shut the light off.

She went to look out the living room window. At the back of her mind, elsewhere in the house, she could hear the children moving around, doing their normal routine for a weeknight. If they spoke to each other then it was only in a murmur. This was one of those nights when no one talked loud.

Her head hung and a blow of air left her lips, a long sigh. She walked away from the window, away from looking into the dark night. She went to call him. This would be the fourteenth call she had made.

"Hey, you reached me, but you didn't catch me. Try again."

The jovial message that she heard for the fourteenth time tonight was a message she had been hearing for thirty years.

*

10:45 p.m. She had decided to settle down and watch some of the shows she had recorded. Miranda came in while the credits were rolling on a sitcom.

"I'm going to bed, Mom. Daniel is going to be up for a

while, he has work to do for school, so he told me to tell you goodnight."

Miranda came and sat next to her mom and gave one of her signature hugs.

"He will be fine, Mom, he always comes back."

Amelia said, "I know, honey, but still I wish, I wish, I wish I knew for sure that's all, honey."

Miranda was talking as Amelia looked at the clock on the wall, not really paying any attention to what she was saying. 11:15 p.m. She looked at her daughter, smiled and kissed her baby panda, Miranda. That was her nickname for her. Even though Miranda was about to start a PhD, Amelia still liked calling her Panda. Amelia also loved to sing the Barry Manilow song "Can't Smile Without You", and she always dedicated it to her son Daniel. These two silly things she would never give up doing, and secretly she knew her adorable, lovable kids didn't want her to stop.

Miranda went away to her room. After a while Amelia switched the TV off with a jab of the remote and made her way to the master bedroom suite. There was still a line of light at the bottom of Daniel's door. She smiled, lightly knocked.

"Night, Dan."

He responded in kind.

First thing in the master bedroom, she looked at the clock on the night table. 11:22 p.m. She sat on the bed.

Where can he be!

*

The normal nightly routine. Brushed her teeth, changed into

night clothes, got into bed. She stretched to turn off the light on the night table. The bedside clock read 11:50 p.m. She shook her head and rested it on the pillow.

He had been pulling stunts like this all their married life. It was his thing, his M.O. Running away, always trying to get away from something rather than face it. She had thought that he would get better the older he got but it was getting worse. Especially over these last few years. It was like the younger version of himself had built up walls around his past, and they had worked to protect him most of the time, and he still trusted in them, but they were eroding with time and age and he didn't have the resources to keep patching them up. All he could do was shrink himself down, try to squeeze into the safety of their ever-receding cover, and keep kidding himself the walls were working.

One last sigh. She turned on her side and tried to sleep. Her eyes were closed but her mind was not clear. She couldn't sleep. Her last thought at 12:15 a.m. was, "Please, God, bring him home safe."

*

Slam. Amelia opened her eyes. 2:25 a.m. She must have fallen asleep. Quickly, she got out of bed, poked her head into the hallway.

"Honey, is that you?"

No answer. Amelia went to the door of the kitchen, completely dark except for the streetlights that came through the windows. She peered into the darkness, towards the door that led from the garage. A darker rectangle on a dark wall, and a man-shaped outline slumped next to it.

"Honey? Are you OK? Do you want me to get you anything? Are you hungry?"

"No." He answered firmly and loudly.

She closed her eyes, silently thanking God he had come back again. This time.

But what about the next time? She decided not to think about the next time for now.

"Honey, let's just go to bed, OK?"

Her eyes were adjusting. She could see him look up. She couldn't see his eyes but he would be looking into hers.

"OK." He reached out an arm and their hands touched. His skin was freezing. Fingers twined slowly around each other, signaling, communicating in ways their owners couldn't manage with words.

Slowly he rose to his feet. They held on tight and gently hugged each other. Amelia felt tears on his face, but didn't say a word. Just allowed him to quietly cry. Then she led him to their bedroom. She glanced at the bottom of Daniel's door as they passed by. He still had the lights on. Had he heard his father's return? He showed no signs of coming out to see.

In their room she made Nick sit down on their bed, talking in a low voice to guide him while she helped him undress. He sat dazed, looking down at the floor, making the minimum movements needed to help her change him from day clothes to bed clothing.

"Do you want to use the bathroom before going to sleep?"

He shook his head, no, so she put him into bed with the blankets over him and gently stroked his head. He was out in a matter of seconds.

She looked down at his freezing face, his cold body, tried to make sure he was covered well. There were no more smiles on her face. Cool, slow sighs passed between her lips. She stayed, staring, for a good minute. Then she went to her side of the bed and got in quietly, turned over, made herself comfortable. And though she tried to squeeze her eyes shut to stop it, tears started to roll down her face. She closed her eyes, blinking, wiping the tears with her fingers as best she could. She reached for some tissues to try and blow her nose quietly. Then she put them back on the night table and took a deep breath. With the back of her hand, she cleaned the tears from her cheeks again.

She tried to make herself comfortable again, all the while thinking, "Thank God he's back home."

She knew with all her heart, soul and mind that something must be done. But what? She had no idea how to get into mental health therapy. She guessed that finding a doctor would be easy. It was getting him to realize that he needed to see this type of doctor that would be the challenge. He was stubborn – he would never admit he needed help.

She looked down to the foot of the bed, where Barney was comfortably sleeping. She smiled and rubbed his back. Without lifting his head, he decided to waggle his tail.

"Barney, how can we help Daddy feel better?" she asked softly. She let out a long sigh and took one more look at her husband. "Sweetheart, I wish I knew how to help you better."

Finally, she fell asleep herself.

CHAPTER 9

*H*ONKKKKKKKKK. The loud blast of a car horn. Not aimed at me because I'm not in the car. I shake my head and return to Earth.

I look around, left and right, not knowing where I am. I am sitting on a bench a short distance from the road in the park, the same park where Amelia and Barney and I enjoy walking. This time I am alone. I am in my signature position, my long legs stretched out, my hands in my pockets, pushing my coat down toward the ground. My head turned down, my eyes wide open, it's like everyone and everything is living around me while I am stuck, paralyzed, to the bench.

I have no memory of how long I have been sitting there. Not realizing that I have been out for a couple hours. Not realizing life all around me is moving at a normal pace. All kinds of traffic on the streets, cars hustling back home with people who worked today. Cops driving by on patrol. The two cars that nearly enjoyed a rear-ender are pulling away from each other, fists waving out of windows and faint shouts of "Asshole!" drifting in the cool evening air. A world closing up the day with just one thing on everyone's mind and that is to get home. To get to where they have made a nest of their own little peace of mind.

I only remember telling Daniel I would be home later and not to wait for me for dinner. I look at my cell phone and see the time is 6:45 p.m. They must be finished with dinner by now. I notice fourteen missed calls from Amelia but nothing indicating a message. She knows me well enough not to leave one. I get up and start walking around, not even thinking, just walking. I have no idea at this point, I just walk.

The cold air reminds us all how the season is changing, so we need to adapt. That's a great word, right? That is what we do, we adapt to survive. It gets cold so we put on extra clothing. It snows, we need boots. It rains, we need an umbrella. All things we do as humans living minute to minute, trying to adapt to life's circumstances, to adjust to anything so we can live a happy life.

I look at my cell phone to see that the time is 6:49 p.m.

*

I notice that I am in the vicinity of the laundromat, so I decide to go inside. It should be nice and warm, I think.

I push the door open and I am shocked to see how busy it really is at this time of day. All the machines are working, people are all over. Who is loading, who is unloading, who is getting ready to collect their things? A whole world inside a world in this small space. I even get ticked off when I see someone using my machines, sitting in my chair at the back. I think, how dare they take over my space. Silly, right? Even stupid.

I blow into my cupped hands to warm them up.

"Look, Mac, move your ass, I got a lot of loads here need folding."

It's Bertha, half a lit cigarette hanging from her mouth, her hair disheveled in a big mess, though she is by nature a very tidy person. She is also a very hard-working person. You get the feeling the owner is happy that she is the manager but no one, including the owner, gets in her way, as she makes clear to all.

"Hi Bertha, I was in the area, so I decided to just come in, get warmed up." I add, "Don't you know you're not allowed to smoke, especially in laundromats?"

"Yeah, I know that." Just by speaking, she blows smoke into my face. I wave it away with my hand and cough. She says, "Excuse me, I got to get this done. This is my last load of folding." She throws a big pullover jersey that looks like it belonged to a quarterback footballer. It hits me like a football being tossed in a Hail Mary pass to me, and I say, "UGH!"

She says, "Give me a hand and help me get this done."

*

I follow her to the space next to her office. It is filled with plastic bags neatly packed with sorted laundry, with names to indicate the family to pick it up. I lay the jersey on the counter and start to fold it in what feels like the right way. Immediately she yells at me, "*No*, not that way. Look, Mac, don't make more work for me."

I do as she tells me – it is better than dealing with her ranting and raving. We are both folding when she says, "What are you doing in this neck of the woods?"

I look around at everyone busy doing their own thing. I tell her, "I just needed to go for a walk." She blows her cigarette smoke in my face again. Finally, she stubs the cigarette out. I say to her, "Well, I am glad you're done smoking." She says, "So are my doctors." She laughs, hits me on the back and goes into her office, letting me finish folding the assigned clothing.

I finish the last piece of clothing, put the appropriate sticker on the plastic bag and stow it along with the other items stacked neatly.

"Well, you did a good job, if I say so myself." She sits down at her desk. I sit in the empty chair in her office. I look at my cell phone. 8:10 p.m.

I say, "What time do you work till?"

"It all closes at 9 p.m. I work from 6 a.m. till nine p.m., every day except Sunday. I don't work on Sunday, that's the Lord's Day and I keep it sacred. If the owner wants this place open in Sunday's best, they get over and open it up."

I have a feeling the owner doesn't mind conceding to this demand. The place looks well taken care of, making him a lot of extra cash, following her rules.

We sit in her office, just talking about anything. About the season changing and about politics. About all these new ideas, about changes occurring in the world. Some things we agree on and other things we decide we best not talk about, if we want to stay friends. You can tell she has had a tough life, meaning nothing ever was handed to her. She still is a decent, honest person, maybe a little rough around the edges but still a decent person.

I notice it is past 9 p.m. and the place is empty. She gathers her stuff, turns off the light, puts the alarm on and we head out. She locks the door, puts an unlit cigarette in her mouth and says, "Need a lift home?" I tell her I don't live that far. We say good night and we go our different ways.

*

I have noticed that whenever I am distracted, my life goes back to that zombie zone. That zone of being fucked-up in a way that ruins my life.

I keep on walking, passing Greens Restaurant. It is a nice neighborhood bar and restaurant. A respectable place where you can bring your wife and children. I look at my cell: the time shows 10 p.m. I walk inside and order a beer with hamburger and fries. I am so hungry, I eat like I haven't eaten for a week. I drink four beers and suddenly it is 2 a.m., which is closing time at Greens. I pay my bill and gather my things and head home, in the cold, hands in my pockets. I am thinking this whole evening was a bust. All that wasted time that I could have enjoyed with my family. And Amelia will get pissed when she sees the credit card bill from Greens.

*

I am half blasted drunk, and half consumed with what Nicholas shared with me today. I drop my keys. Now I know I am wasted. I pick them up and make my way into the kitchen. I hear Barney's paws clicking over the floor towards me. He looks at me as if to say, "Where the hell were you?" I pick him up and give him a hug. He forgives me and wags his tail. I put Barney back down, close the door and lock it.

I must have passed out, because when I open my eyes, I see Amelia with her hand held out to me. The next thing

I remember is sleeping warmly in my bed. I wake up, look around. The clock says 5:35 a.m. I look to my right. Amelia is sleeping. I put my head back on my pillow and I am out.

*

I wake up late that morning. When I sit up, my head feels like it is going to explode. Barney is sleeping at the foot of the bed and he lifts up his own head. He always brings a smile into my mornings. I love that dog so much. I hope he knows how much happiness he brings to my family's life.

I make my way into the kitchen to get something to eat so I can take my morning medications. I start to feel better from the hangover, which means I think back to how I was feeling, which means I remember why I was feeling that way, and I start to think again about Nicholas's mugging. I cannot get the image out of my mind of Nicholas in a headlock, dragged into a men's room stall. My hand pets the top of Barney's head while I look through the window out at nothing.

"How big is his school, Barney, do you think?" I say quietly. His tail just thumps the floor at the sound of his name.

"How could no one see what was happening to him?"

Thump, thump, thump.

"Or maybe they did." Which is worse, because now I'm seeing all those kids just standing by, watching and no one helping while what happens, happens.

"What a world we live in."

CHAPTER 10

As usual, Nicholas sat at the back, alone, trying to be invisible, just wanting to get to school without incident.

It was the usual mixture of people on the bus, on the usual route around town. It was around 7 a.m. so as usual this included teenage children. Nicholas's least favourite kind of guys.

He shrank back even further into his seat as the bus drew up to the stop. Through the window he could see the bunch of kids, waiting. All boys. If he was extra still then maybe they wouldn't notice him in return. The bus picked up the newcomers, closed its doors, and moved along on its route.

The group of kids, that Nicholas still hoped to remain invisible from, made their way back to where he was sitting. He gazed downwards, trying not to make eye contact. Trying to exist separately to them, in a place where they couldn't possibly feel threatened or challenged by him. He was aware of them beside him, looking down.

There was no preliminary, no challenge, no warm-up, no statement of intentions. They just went about their business as if this was their routine, the sole reason they had boarded the bus in the first place. He felt two powerful fists grasp hold of the fabric of his hoodie. Then they hauled him from his seat and dragged him to the very back of the bus, with laughing and foul words being yelled out loud. They laid him out flat on the back seat and other fists started to land. Powerful, pounding all over, the shock and pain driving the breath from his body while he tried to hold on to his backpack, his hoodie, his dignity.

"Asshole!"

"Dickhead!"

"Mother fucker!"

"Queer!" Each pair of fists had a wonderful vocabulary of expletives attached to it. He never saw any of their faces. He had pulled the hood over his head to block his view of their intentions. The laughing grew louder.

As usual, no one came to help him. They could have been the only people on the bus. Every bystander made the same excuse to themselves: "Why should I get involved? Not my problem, not my place." If you ignored it, if you didn't hear or see it, then it didn't exist.

They must have reached the stop where the pairs of fists were headed because the pounding stopped. The jeers and laughter were at their loudest and still no one moved to help him. But the torment wasn't quite over. Inside his hood, Nicholas felt them take hold of his body and hoist him into the air. The weight in his skull told him he was hanging upside down.

He felt them fumbling around his feet and then his whole weight was on his ankles, dangling from the grab handles attached to the ceiling.

Nicholas heard the doors hiss open, the laughs and the jeers turning into normal teen boy voices that receded as their owners got off. The doors closed again, the bus headed off.

The bus driver finally looked in the mirror and let himself see. He jammed the brakes on and brought the bus to a halt.

"Oh my God! Someone come help me!"

Two men finally allowed themselves to notice what the bus driver had seen, and ran to assist him. Still inside his hood, Nicholas waved his hands as he swung upside down, jerking his body, trying to do something to help himself. He felt the three pairs of hands take his weight, trying to free him. His legs and feet swung down to the floor of the bus as soon as they had freed his ankles. At last he could pull his hood back and emerge blinking into the daylight, his vision blurred by tears. Nicholas dropped to the floor the moment the men let go of him. Grown men's faces gazed down at him, stamped with the shock and concern they had totally failed to show a minute earlier. One of them had some loose belts dangling in his hand. The kids had used their own belts to perform this fun escapade. They hadn't even cared about leaving them behind. They just wanted to pull off this prank so they could gloat happily over it all day at school. Cost of a new belt, ten bucks. Beating up a helpless kid and hanging him from the ceiling, priceless.

The humiliation peaked under their stares. Nicholas leapt up and grabbed his bag and ran to the doors without stopping to thank the men, but as the driver was away from his seat and the bus was parked, the doors were locked shut. He pushed on the door, then banged, then shoved, hammering on the glass with both fists like a trapped animal in a corner. All he could think about was getting off the bus, getting out of the situation, finding a place to hide. The driver ran back to his seat to press the switch and give the crazy trapped animal kid his freedom. The doors folded themselves open and Nicholas went flying down to the sidewalk. Running to freedom, running to keep his dignity, running for safety. All he thought about.

Unexpectedly the bus had dropped him off near his sanctuary. He could see it ahead and he ran straight to it, not thinking of anything else but to go inside, hide and try to get his head straight.

He crashed through the door, panting, and now that he knew he was safe he fell to his knees, sobbing.

*

I go in to the laundromat and as usual a cloud of smoke engulfs me. It seems thicker and stronger than usual. I call hello to Bertha and I hear another voice laughing with her. I find her with another woman in her office, both smoking their brains out.

I say, "Hi Bertha, how are you?"

"Hey, Mac," she replies, "this is my sister, Blanche."

"Blanche and Bertha, how goes it today?" I asked.

They both roar with laughter. The air is thick with smoke.

"Listen, dummy," says Bertha, "don't forget to press them buttons to get the machine working as I showed you."

"I won't, Bertha. Thanks for your kind advice."

I drag my laundry bag over to my favorite spot, the back right hand side of the room, and I get the machine all set and ready to go. I set down in my favorite chair, stretch my long legs out and shake my head, smiling. Bertha and Blanche, what a pair. Peas in a pod.

I close my eyes, sink into the white noise of the washing machine. About five minutes pass, and over the sound of the machine, I hear weeping. I open my eyes, look over at the back room. I get up, go to the door, peer over to the dark corner. I see Nicholas slumped on his knees, facing into the corner where the walls meet, shoulders shaking with sobs.

"Nicholas, is that you? Are you OK?"

He gets up. Not looking at me. He looks anywhere else but into my eyes.

I say, "What happened to you?"

I glance over at Bertha's office. Maybe she'll come over. I see Bertha looking out at me. Then she punches her sister's arm.

"He's at it again, talking back there." She shakes her head and goes back to her seat. I look back at Nicholas.

"What happened?" I ask again.

He speaks, and as he recounts his tale of horror, my head fills with images, each worse than the one before. Just as I am wrapping my brain cells around one mental picture, along comes the next, piling into it, knocking it away and demanding attention for itself. A train wreck of pictures in my mind.

I picture this kid strung upside down, hanging from the bus's ceiling. And no one even tried to intervene until after it was all done? They all waited till the end, till the rotten kids ran out of the bus. Why didn't anyone do something sooner?

When he has finished, I let out a long sigh. I escort him to a chair next to mine. I comfort him as best I can, try to help him make sense, but I can't make sense of it myself. The washer goes from cycle to cycle. Time never stops, it just keeps going forward. I keep thinking how he went through that horrible ordeal.

I hear the machine going into its final phase. It will spin to a halt in a moment and I stand up ready for it. I glance back at him. His lonely eyes look straight ahead and they are filled with tears. He gets up slowly and walks to the front of the store. I see him peek out, first left then right, then walk out.

Just at that point, the washer comes to a loud stop. I shake my head and wipe the tears from my own face, then make my way to the washer and prepare the clothing for the dryer. I go back to my seat. My head falls into my hands as I think, "What a fucked-up world we live in."

Bertha and Blanche have finished another cigarette by now and have folded the clothing into plastic bags. They are talking to each other as I stay seated, thinking more and more about Nicholas's story. Then I sit up and sit back and blow out, puffing my cheeks. Have I turned a corner? I remember how I reacted to the tale of Nicholas's mugging in the bathroom. But this time feels different. I seem to have it under control.

When everything is finally done, I gather all my stuff to leave. As I walk out of the place I yell, "Take care, Bertha, and nice meeting you, Blanche."

They both yell "Goodbye" in sync. As I pull the door shut behind me, I hear Bertha turn to Blanche and say, "He's a strange one!" They both chuckle and smoke their cigarettes as I walk to my car.

*

I pull up in the driveway and go into the house, the laundry in a folded pile on top of both my arms. I see Daniel's bike in the garage, so he's already home. As I come up to his room I hear his music blasting through his door. Well, let the kid relax whichever way works.

Something catches my foot. I stumble forward and everything in my arms goes flying.

He has left his sneakers lying outside his door. I get up, grab his shoes and pace to his room. Banging on the door like a maniac. Daniel opens the door with a smile, and suddenly I am screaming so loud you might have thought the house was on fire. The kid doesn't know what's hit him.

"My feet were all tied up! I fell over! Because you left your shoes in the way!"

I am screaming ready to kill him and he just stands there looking at me, eyes wide.

"Sorry, Dad, I'm really sorry." His usual temperament, polite and quiet. It just winds me up more. He should be hating, hurting like me.

"Sorry? You're sorry? I could have gotten hurt bad and all you can say is sorry?"

Suddenly Miranda is there and she stands between us, yelling herself.

"STOP IT! JUST STOP IT!"

I quieten down and she continues.

"We are sick and tired of you coming home each day yelling, screaming all the time! There is never peace in this house! We walk around on eggshells, worried you're going to snap! We are sick and tired of this and that's it, we are not taking it anymore!"

Now Daniel is trying to calm both his sister and his father down. They both have the same temperament while he is always the peacemaker. He tries to solve the family wars. His words wash over me. I catch the tone but not the meaning. I look at them both, look at the floor, run my fingers through my hair, walk out of Daniel's room, kick my way through the scattered laundry still lying on the floor, make my way to my bedroom. I slam the door behind me.

*

Miranda and Daniel looked at each other. Then they walked around the house and picked up everything their father had dropped. Folded it, put everything away nicely, made their way to their own bedrooms, slowly closed the doors, without saying a word.

CHAPTER 11

Each of them all in their own space. Each of them not knowing what just happened.

Daniel smashed himself on his bed. Spreading out, lying on his back, hands behind his head, legs out and looking at the ceiling with a long exhaling sigh.

"Oh, Dad, how much longer...?"

He closed his eyes, slowed his breathing.

It was a trick he had learned forever ago. He couldn't remember when. Just that when his Dad was standing inches in front of him – and towering over him, as he had done when Daniel was little – and ranting and raging, Daniel could withdraw. His body stayed where it was but his mind pulled back. He went into a safe space, a locked room inside, where he could look out at the little boy just standing there, and the angry man whose mouth was flapping up and down and not realizing that his words were just empty hot air.

Perspective. That was the trick.

That dad back at the gym. Daniel had thought he had the guy pegged, a boorish and unpleasant man, until the guy had abruptly turned the tables like that. No, he really had not expected it to turn out like that.

Daniel worked in a school so he got to deal with a lot of

parents. All of humanity was reflected there. Some of them had their problems. In his not very long time as a trainee teacher he had already known two kids report that they no longer lived with both Mom and Dad, and in one case it was because Dad couldn't keep his fists to himself. In fact it had started when another teacher had noticed bruises that the girl tried to hide. Now, that Mom and Dad weren't just separated. There was a court order in place preventing the Dad from ever coming close to his children without an official escort, and never to their house at all.

Though Daniel knew it wasn't always that way around. All the staff had had training on how to recognise domestic abuse. Sometimes it was the Mom who did the abusing.

If there had ever been physical violence in their own home, in the Rato household, if any of them had ever carried physical bruises from a physical assault – well, then, Daniel didn't know what he would have done. He wouldn't hesitate to defend Miranda or Mom if he needed to, from Dad, or from anyone. He was big enough to hit back now, if he ever had to, though he knew it would destroy them all if it ever came to that.

But for all his faults, Dad was never violent. That was the only reason Daniel's mind trick could work. Dad's fists were his words. They could bruise the soul but never the body. Sometimes, just sometimes there were veiled hints of why that might be. Daniel was pretty certain Dad had known violence when he was younger, violence against him, and maybe that was why he never used it on anyone else.

Just his rage. Just his words. Daniel could deal with that.

Except that it took energy. A great deal of it. When he had

been younger with infinite reserves of energy to draw upon, he hadn't realized just how much it used up. But as he grew older, he had realized his reserves took longer and longer to replenish.

Put another way, putting up with Dad took more and more out of him. And one day those reserves would be gone, and he lived in quiet dread of the day he could no longer cope.

*

"Who does he think he is? I mean, we try to live our lives and he still acts as if we are little..."

Miranda had locked her door and she stood in the middle of a pile of all her things.

"There is always some bug up his ass..."

She had started to put her things away, but nothing was right in the room. If she wanted to put something down then she had to move something to somewhere else, and then that somewhere else needed to be cleared of whatever was already there.

"Well, I am tired of that bug. I am tired of being his punching bag. I am not taking it anymore..."

At first she had merely moved Object A (maybe a book) to Location B (maybe a shelf) to make a space for Item C (maybe a photo or a bit of clothing). But as she went on, she grew more and more tired and bored and fed up of shifting stuff about, and her movements become more and more disorganized and violent, until she was throwing armfuls of her belongings about everywhere and now here she was, with all her worldly goods and possessions heaped around her.

She stood with her hands on her hips and gazed around. Well, maybe the room had been due a cleaning anyway. Calmer now, she began to put things back to where they should be, while she carried on talking out loud to herself.

"That's it. I am done and soon as Mom comes home, I am going to tell her."

She was preparing her speech as she got her things together, as if she was talking to a class, lecture style, laying out the formula. Word by word, phrase by phrase, line by line she was building up what she was going to say to Mom.

Miranda stopped for a moment, head cocked. A sound you could barely hear, unless you were used to it. Was that the door...? She heard Barney's claws scrabbling on the kitchen floor, and a series of happy, yapping barks. And then it was confirmed. Mom's voice: "Hi, everyone, I'm home."

This was it, Miranda thought. Her chance to put her foot down and finally break free. She grabbed her door handle to her room and pulled – forgetting she had locked it.

It took half a second to unlock it, long enough to reflect that freedom comes in many forms. Getting out of her room was only the first step towards a greater freedom. Freedom from this abusive animal of a father she and Daniel called Dad and Mom called Honey. The beast that lived among them all. They were all locked up with a caged animal. They huddled together in the center of the cage and it paced around them, no one ever knowing when it would suddenly attack. Always making them feel uncomfortable, unwanted, right in their own home. Home! The place you should look forward to going to at the end of your day. That place didn't exist for her, Daniel or Mom.

Well, Miranda told herself as she stormed from her room, she was going to tell Mom enough is enough. This was her liberation day. Not only for her but for Daniel and her mother too.

*

Mom was hugging Barney as Miranda came blazing in. She heard Miranda mumbling under her breath and she smiled up.

"Hi, Honey, how was your..."

Miranda let fly before Amelia could get one sentence out.

"Mom, I am done! This is it! Dad comes home screaming and yelling at Dan. You know Dan. He just listens to Dad, taking it all in. I just walked in and that *thing*, that *animal* you married and call Honey, is berating Dan, and Dan and I are sick and tired of coming home to this... *beast!*"

Amelia recognized her daughter was on a roll. She slowly stood up from the dog. Barney failed to get the cue and didn't understand why the cuddles had stopped. He stood on his hind legs, resting his paws against Amelia's knees, looking up and wagging his tail hopefully. Amelia absently tickled the top of his head to keep him happy, and let Miranda speak.

She was listening to every word, but she knew this speech by heart. She had heard Miranda talk like this a week ago. A month. A year. A thousand times before. The speech was on full blast with new examples, but the rhetoric was always the same.

This time, though, Amelia noticed a change in Miranda's delivery. Her voice a little closer to the edge, her breathing heavier, her eyes wilder. Miranda was pacing, hands waving, sometimes even stumbling slightly as the words jumbled together in her head, fighting for position and only able to get out one by one. Even more upset than usual. This was not one of those situations where she could just say that everything will be fine because in her heart, in her soul, she knew Miranda was right. Her heart was pumping fast because everything Miranda said, she agreed with, one hundred per cent.

Until today, Amelia had always felt that things would fix themselves. She had always hoped that a solution would surface and rid this family of the problem with their father's abusive behavior.

But when she looked at Miranda with a mother's eyes, she saw a young woman who had no more to give. Of the three of them, it was Miranda who had finally reached the end first. Amelia had dreaded this day. She knew it was inevitable, though she had always hoped it wouldn't come.

The worst part of all of this was that when Miranda finished her rant, solutions would be needed.

At last, after minutes or hours, Miranda slowed down and stopped, every word spent. She stared at her mother in mute and helpless appeal. Amelia opened her arms and Miranda walked into them.

"It's just not fair, Mom." Amelia could feel her daughter trembling with shakes that weren't quite sobs, and the fabric of her shirt growing damp with Miranda's tears. Barney was jumping up and down again, demanding attention, and over Miranda's shoulder Amelia saw Dan's six-foot two-inch frame fill the door, his hands in his pockets. He wore a gentle smile but his eyes were dark and hurting. Amelia made a gesture of greeting while still consoling Miranda. Daniel came forward and stood with them, hands in pockets, just outside of hugging range but every bit a part of this family huddle.

Barney yapped and all three of them looked down. He beamed up at them, his tail pounding the floor, and it broke the tension and they all started to laugh.

"Let's sit," Amelia suggested.

*

In a strange way they all felt a sense of relief. Amelia, Daniel, Miranda and even Barney all knew this day was long overdue. From this day forward, things were going to be different.

Somehow.

They sat at the kitchen table, and looked at each other, and without saying a word their eyes knew what they felt inside their hearts, souls and their minds.

Miranda was the first to speak, even though she had already said it all to Amelia, and Daniel knew it all too well because he had been there. But it felt more formal – not just pouring out anger and frustration but setting the agenda. Laying out the basis for a plan of action, whatever that might be. Daniel did not mind giving the stage to his sister. The less he had to talk was fine with him. All he had to do was to give confirmation that what she was saying was correct.

"Uh-huh..."

"Yup..."

"That's it..."

Amelia knew that Miranda would give a truthful narrative of events but Daniel still gave his positive confirmation. It made this a meeting of minds, all contributing their thoughts. They all sat there contemplating what to do next with "the animal". Amelia didn't like them referring to their father in that manner but for now she left it alone. She knew deep down they loved him. They just wanted to find the love to make the right decision.

Amelia stretched her right hand out to Daniel and her left to Miranda. Barney was under the table next to her feet. She smiled, reassuring them, giving them emotional support. She took a deep breath and spoke.

"What do you think should be done?"

She wanted this to be a mutual decision. A decision that they all thought would benefit not only their lives but would help "the animal".

Daniel puffed out his cheeks.

"He's got to get help, Mom."

"Why? Why can't he just deal with it?" Miranda demanded.

"We could talk about it together, as a family..." Amelia suggested.

"So he can explode at all of us at once? Maybe Dan's idea is best."

"Yeah, but come to think of it I don't know I want to get anyone else involved..."

Round and round they went. The same ideas coming up and then maybe even the same person seeing the flaw in the idea and coming round to someone else's idea. Over and over. All viable tactics, but which one to use?

Somehow the three of them circled into a decision. Whatever happened, someone had to talk to Dad. To let him know how they all felt – and also get his own input. One thing they all knew was, there was no forcing him. If he didn't want it then nothing was going to happen. And since a family scene would just wind him up, and maybe lead to more casualties, there was only one person who could do it. They all agreed in the end that it was probably best if Mom went to his room, their private master suite, alone and made some really hard decisions with him.

Amelia squeezed both her children's hands, pushed back her chair, and set off physically and mentally to their bedroom. She reached the door, took a deep breath, held the door handle just for a second. It felt like an eternity. She turned the handle ever so gently and walked slowly in.

She stopped in her tracks and her eyes opened wide, in shock.

CHAPTER 12

For a moment, an actual moment, she thought he had taken his own life. Or just dropped dead, of a heart attack or a stroke or an aneurysm. He sat slumped on the floor as though every muscle in his body had gone, his back against the bed, his face turned away. A broken man.

But then his head moved, and her heart slowed down and she could breathe again. Amelia's hands were in a prayer position, touching her chin and lips.

Amelia had been rehearsing the words to say but now she just dropped them. This wasn't the time for speaking. She slowly walked closer as he sat looking straight ahead, away from her gaze. Gently, slowly, Amelia sat next to him. Her left hand moved closer to his right, gently touched him. He did not move. Amelia positioned her hand to hold his and he accepted it. She gazed at him until he slowly turned his head towards her and their eyes met. He looked away, then back to Amelia. They looked at each other for what felt like an eternity. No words were spoken, just eyes gazing at each other. Silent tears poured down his face. He looked slowly away again while she kept her eyes on the profile of his face. They stayed like this for what seemed to be a lifetime.

"They want to know why, Honey. They want to understand so badly."

No answer. He continued to gaze ahead.

"Have you ever told them?" she asked softly. The tiniest movement of his head. Maybe shaking it, no. She opened her mouth to say it again, but he spoke, the softest whisper, air barely moving in his throat.

"They know."

It wasn't an answer, so this time she did say it again.

"Have you ever *told* them?"

A very long pause. His lips barely moved.

"No."

"You should."

"No..."

"They will never understand, Honey. They want to. But you have to give them something to hang it on."

He spoke a little more loudly.

"They can tr-..."

The words choked off. He bit back a sob and looked away. He couldn't say it, and he couldn't say the reason why he couldn't, because they all knew it. They were a long way past the point of "They can trust me".

"Honey, they have to know."

"I..." He swallowed. Adam's apple bobbing up and down. "I can't say it. It was hard enough telling you."

But they both knew she was right.

Amelia thought a little more. Then she reached into her pocket and pulled out her phone. She opened the contacts with a tap, scrolled to the name she had in mind, angled the phone so that he could see it. Raised one eyebrow in query. He turned his head just enough to let his eyes flick over the screen, and after a moment he gave the minutest, tiniest nod before he looked away again.

Good enough, Amelia thought as she slipped the phone back into her pocket. He had understood her suggestion, and that tiny nod counted as approval.

*

Daniel and Miranda looked at the closed door of their parents' room.

Miranda went first.

"You think we should go in there?"

"I don't think that's a good idea. Let's leave them alone for a while."

"Well, I'm hungry..."

Their chairs scraped backwards.

They worked together to make a quick and easy meal. Chopping up onions and garlic, frying mince while the pasta cooked. Daniel took a plate to go sit in front of the TV in the den. Miranda stayed eating at the counter and looking over her homework.

It was all displacement activity for the same thing on both their minds. Every now and then they shot another look at the closed door. What was happening between Mom and Dad?

*

She had helped him to get undressed again. They both knew the motions. They each had a part in this play that was getting

Dad into bed because he had had another bad day and needed to be put to sleep.

No words at all, this time. He slipped neatly into bed and Amelia gently covered him. She went to kiss the top of his head but then decided not to. His eyes were already closed and he didn't notice. Ever so gently she stroked his hair and forehead. She hoped that he would fall quickly to sleep. She shut the light off and gently closed the door.

She stood outside, looking down at the floor, not moving an inch. Both hands again in a prayer-like position by her chin, lips and nose. Her mind was in a thousand places, thinking of a thousand things. She needed to join the kids in the kitchen, so she started to walk, and then she cracked and almost started to sob hysterically. She quickly stopped herself. Stood still again. Took a deep breath, stood up straight, pressed her top, rubbed her pants clean. She tried to straighten her clothing and body to an acceptable position to enter a room and seem like everything was fine. She accomplished it with solid determination as she walked into the kitchen with her signature smile.

"Daddy's gone to bed; you know how tired he gets from his medicines."

Daniel was always accepting and never prying; Miranda's mind was still clicking with thoughts.

"So, the animal is fine now. Did he calm down or tell you why he went nuts on us today?"

Amelia said, "Miranda, please, I'm sure he didn't go nuts – right, Dan?"

This was usually where Daniel's answers were on the positive side. This time he was honest.

"No, Ma, he was a little out of control."

"What!" Miranda exclaimed. "A little? He was nuts, Dan!"

Amelia saw the plates on the side. Good, the kids had eaten.

"Come to the table, both of you. We're going to make a call."

*

The three of them sat together on one side of the table, with the laptop set up where they could all see it. Amelia reached out and clicked the cursor over "Join Now".

She glanced at her children while the buffering wheel span. They couldn't take their eyes from the screen. Dan's jaw was set, his teeth clenched tight. Miranda was slowly working her mouth from side to side. They were both nervous, she realized. Maybe even frightened. They had asked for the truth. Knowing you're going to get it can suddenly be a terrifying thing.

And then there was a man on screen, looking like he could be Nick's brother, though instead of dark, his hair was blonde turning to gray, and he still sported the designer stubble of his youth. But when he grinned at them all, teeth flashing, it was the full-on family smile beaming out at them from the west coast.

"Hey, guys!"

Miranda and Daniel smiled and lifted a hand to wave.

"Hey, Uncle Tony."

The man on the screen had always been Uncle Tony when they were little, though in fact they were first cousins once removed. His mother and their grandfather were brother and sister. They didn't see a lot of each other, living on opposite sides of the country, but they kept in touch.

Uncle Tony's cheery smile turned serious.

"So, your Mom tells me that she and your Dad want me to tell you..."

"We don't need to do small talk," Miranda interrupted. "Why does Dad go nuts like that?"

"He went nuts, huh?" Tony asked quietly.

"Again," Miranda confirmed. Uncle Tony's eyes shifted to Amelia.

"I didn't catch how bad this was."

"It's as bad as it's ever been, Tony. And – he just can't say it to his own kids. He just can't. There's this block inside him. And I only know what he's told me, which I don't think is anything like everything. There's only one person who knows anything like the whole story, and that's you. You were there when he was growing up."

"Well, yeah. But remember I'm two years younger than him. Even I didn't see that much."

Amelia felt a stab of doubt. This had seemed such a good idea. Bypass her husband's mental block – with his permission – by going to someone who could say the things they needed to know freely. But if Tony didn't actually know... She hoped she hadn't raised the children's expectations too high.

"He said he told you stuff," she persisted. On screen, Tony shrugged.

"I don't think he ever told me the half of it. If that. Just a fraction. But if you want to hear that little..."

"Yes," they all said at the same time.

Another shrug.

"Okay. Let's see. Well, there was this time..."

Tony talked for maybe ten minutes while no one interrupted, and Amelia felt the world shifting around them. Patterns emerging, dots connecting, things falling into place. She could see it in her children's eyes. They might not understand fully but they would never see the world the same way again. Everything that happened to them from now on would be seen and interpreted in light of this information.

At last Tony stopped talking and he sat patiently at the other end of the call, eyes darting from one face to the other while they each processed what they had just heard.

Miranda went first. Her hands waved in front of her, fists clenching and unclenching as if she wanted to seize hold of the truth and pull it out of the thin air.

"Why?" she blurted. "Why why why why why would anyone do that, why?"

"Why? I think that is the answer he's been looking for all these years. There isn't a reason that makes sense. You ask me, I don't think even the kids who did it to him could tell you."

"Children can be little shits," Daniel said quietly.

"True, Dan, and I guess you'd know in your job, but most children manage to be little shits without being little shits in exactly this way."

"Maybe they did it because they could?" Amelia suggested.

"Sure, they *could*," Tony agreed. "Anyone *could*. I *could* walk out of this room this minute and do that to my own kids, or burn the house down, or throw all my clothes off and run down the street. I *could* – but I'm not going to."

Miranda was still making her clutching gestures.

"But," she blurted, "but, why can't he just... just... Why can't he just *get over it?* I mean, sure, it was terrible, it was horrible, but it was a long time ago. No one's out to get him now. He knows that. Why can't he just... be better?"

"Not that simple, sweetheart," Tony said. "This was his teens, remember. It's a time when your whole brain starts rewiring itself and it's immensely sensitive to what's going on around you. If a plant grows up twisted then it stays twisted. It can't just straighten itself out, however much it wants to."

Again, he looked from one face to the other.

"Guys, I'd love to be more help. I really would. But I've told you what I can."

"You've said plenty, Tony," Amelia said softly. "Thank you so much. I don't know what we'll do with it but that's been really helpful."

*

The kids were back in their rooms while Amelia finished cleaning up the kitchen. She dried her hands, put the kitchen towel under the kitchen sink and sat down in the dining area. Her elbows on the table, head resting in her hands. She exhaled slowly as Miranda came in and sat next to her. She reached out a hand; Amelia smiled and took it. They looked quietly at each other.

"So," Miranda said. "We know what we know. What's he going to do about it?"

A deep sigh passed Amelia's lips. "Honey, I don't even know the whole story myself. He's stubborn. I've told him he needs psychiatric help. When I mention this kind of help, he replies, 'I need help?' I've been telling him for years now."

Miranda's face was set, like she was deliberately trying *not* to be sympathetic. Because sympathy would be weakness, and weakness was a luxury none of them could afford.

"I'm glad Tony said what he did, but in the long run, it doesn't make a difference. There's nothing we can do. Only he can. Dan is more tolerant, but I am sick of it. We all have our own crap to deal with."

"Are you still going to leave?" Amelia asked with a smile, which faded as Miranda shot her a hard, cold look. Miranda's threats to move out were old news, had been since her mid-teens. Somehow she was still here. But Amelia wondered if she had pressed it just a bit too far. She did not want Miranda to think that her mother took her feelings lightly.

But Miranda breathed out and looked down at the table.

"No," she said quietly, and Amelia relaxed. Then Miranda looked up from under her brows, and there was a hard resolve there that Amelia hadn't seen before. "Not yet," she added.

CHAPTER 13

It's the middle of the night and I wake up. It's dark and I can hear Amelia sleeping beside me. My memory is blank. I look for the remote in bed. Amelia leaves it for me so when I wake up to use the bathroom, I can turn the TV off. Which is what I do. I make my way to the bathroom and back to bed, and the memories slowly start to come back. I start to recall the bad things I did once again to my children. Memories of my temper flaring, Daniel just standing there tall, Miranda attacking me. I remember being on the floor here in this room when Amelia came home. I remember getting undressed, helped by Amelia and going to bed.

By the time my eyes start to close again, all the horrible details of the evening are vivid in my memories.

"Please someone help me," I think as I once again drift off to sleep.

*

Morning arrives and I can hear the little world in our home getting up to start its normal routines. Amelia, Daniel and Miranda are a mishmash of noises and sounds in the house. I make believe I am asleep. I just don't feel like talking about what happened again last night. I don't even want small talk, not even "How is the weather?" B.S. I stay in bed with my eyes closed and wait until I hear them exiting the house. I have to wait for three exits, three slams of the door and that tiny little change of air pressure in my ears, to make sure I don't confront anyone. The last closing of the door is Daniel. He is always the last to leave because he waits until the last second to get things done. To make sure, I go to the window. I see that Amelia and Miranda's cars are gone, and I get a final glimpse of Daniel on his bike before he turns the corner at the end of the street.

I turn and leave the room. Now it's my turn to do my morning routine.

*

I'm shaved, showered, breakfasted. Taking my last of fifteen medications, I wash the drinking glass and put it away.

I lean against the counter, both hands flat on the cool surface, head resting against the cupboard doors. I breathe out slowly.

I feel bruised. My body is fine but my soul feels like it's gone fifteen rounds with an archangel. "Time heals all things" – that's crap, I'm living testimony to the falseness of that particular adage. "Time is a healer" – yeah, okay, that's true enough as long as what you want to heal isn't that big.

Not enough time has passed since my blow-up yesterday evening. The residue of what happened will take a lot of time to heal.

Your body is meant to know instinctively what it needs. You feel thirsty, you immediately want a glass of water. You binged on the chili last night, today your body knows you only need a light salad. And so on. Well, my body knows it needs peace, and the only place it's going to get it is the laundromat, submerging myself in the soothing white noise of the machines.

Problem: I was there only yesterday and we have nothing to wash. I pick up my coffee and pace about, taking slow sips as I ponder the problem. I head for the bedroom, hold the cup over the bed, tilt my wrist slowly until suddenly there's a dark, wet stain spreading over my king-size bedspread.

Oops, better get that cleaned.

*

So I am on my way, parking my car, gathering up my stuff. As usual, I have the whole place to myself. Walking in I yell out, "Hey Bertha, I'm back." Making my way back to the right-side area of the laundromat I get the washer loaded. I press "start" and as usual it doesn't go on. This time I remember what Boss Bertha said. I bend down and press the appropriate button on the right-hand side and off it goes. I get up and make my way to my favorite chair. Sitting there, my long legs stretched out in front, arms crossed and white noise washing around me. You know you can get any sound you like out of white noise? All the crap in the world is contained in that signal. Well, turns out it absorbs crap too. All the turmoil in my soul is lifting off into the noise that surrounds me.

No sooner has the white noise of the washer helped me enter my world of rest when suddenly I hear a low knocking, knuckles on wood, like they're trying to be heard inside and not out. I open my eyes. Did someone really knock or was it my imagination? A white noise sound hallucination?

Once again, I hear a quiet knock. From the back room? But the door there is open. I look to the front and see Bertha doing her thing, smoking like a bandit and folding clothes into plastic bags. And the front door is all glass so I can see there's no one there.

I go to the back room. I don't see anyone. But there's a back door. I've never seen it used but I guess it opens into the alley behind the row of shops. And there's the knocking again.

I open the door and look around, right and left, and there behind the door I see Nicholas. T-shirt, jeans, hair mussed, hands in pockets, back to the wall.

No words need to be exchanged. I use my hands to gesture to come in and he follows me to my chair. Bertha looks at us from the front and says to herself, "What is he up to now?" between puffs.

Nicholas and I sit down and I look him over. He's agitated. The smallest movements of eyes, of his head, of his body, like he's forever on the very edge of fleeing somewhere. Energy coiled up in that young body, quivering to be released.

"You upset about something?" I say. From the looks of things I have a feeling that he is, but I want him to feel he has permission to speak in his own time.

He is staring at the floor, and it's only because I see his mouth move that I lean closer to hear his answer.

"Yes."

So, I get my body nice and comfortable in the chair, giving my full attention to what he is about to say.

After, I am just in shock. He stays looking at the ground while I look straight ahead, not believing what I just heard.

Every time he tells me these things, I think he's told me the worst. That was how I felt after hearing about his mugging in the bathroom. Nothing could be worse than that.

But unfortunately, something always can be.

What a fucked-up world we live in.

I try to replay the exact events he just shared with me. I am just so sick with disgust but I don't want him to think the disgust is aimed at him. I must take a moment to get my thoughts in order. I close my eyes, take a deep breath. The image is so vivid in my head but it won't settle down for me to look at. I can sense it's there but I only see aspects, facets, clusters of pixels. I can't adjust my viewpoint to take the whole thing in.

The washer is now spinning on full blast.

Nicholas is gone. I blink and look up and see Bertha, staring back at me. She has a look on her face – she is thinking I am nuts. She goes back to smoking, folding clothes and shaking her head. I blink, look down, then I look at the revolving washer, the blur of my bedspread on high spin. My mind is probing what Nicholas just told me, like you probe a sore spot, gradually getting used to the pain, becoming accustomed to it so you can take hold of it. I keep staring into the spinning drum as the events start to come into focus.

CHAPTER 14

"Hey, are you a boy or a girl?"

The yell cut through the clear air of a beautiful day as Nicholas was walking to his weekend job, and straightaway he knew the way this evil spirited confrontation was about to go.

And it was a beautiful day. Blue sky and not a cloud in sight. The park was filled to the max with people enjoying their weekend off, and everyone was having the best time. It was and still is a great family park where the public goes to enjoy and relax. It has its own beach area, a large lake where you can rent paddle boats, a water park with water slides and a concession area selling food. A picture-perfect day with all these fine features – what could possibly be better than that?

The park also has pavilions – large, enclosed areas which a family can rent for the day to have a private party. That weekend the entire lot of pavilions were rented out.

Nicholas had a weekend job in the concession stand, selling pizza, soda, hamburgers, fries, hot dogs, and ice cream. His route to the stand took him past the rented pavilions. He braced himself as they drew near, but then he saw that one of them was full of adults and he let himself relax. Adults didn't care, didn't intervene when their kids were tormenting him, but they didn't initiate it either.

But then some of them moved aside and he saw their children, and he knew he was in trouble. He knew them all, mean-spirited teenagers, all from the same school he attended. And they knew him, the freak of the neighborhood, a reputation bestowed on him without his consent. A reputation he knew all about and desperately tried to hide from his parents and brothers.

First, the teenagers started to yell those horrible comments. "Hey, are you a boy or a girl?" was just one. He picked up his pace, trying to pass this area quickly, but the calls came louder and faster. Relentless in their plan to humiliate him, the teenagers were all pressing to the front of the pavilion, though with a coward's natural instinct they stayed within the safety range of their parents.

"Hey, we're talking to you!"

Now they were confident the parents wouldn't intervene, they started adding expletives. The parents glanced down at them, but looked away again, carried on with their conversations. They must have all noticed what their children were saying and shouting, but they didn't bother to stop them.

One big, football-playing teenager shouted a new variation in a deep, strong voice, "Hey, Fuck Face. You a fuckin' boy or girl?" The yells turned into howls of laughter. The parents didn't even try to silence their children's cruel jibes.

He knew all too well what they meant. He was a small framed child, a little overweight with fat around his chest, making it seem he had man boobs, which he had never even noticed until the first time they kindly called his attention to them. Little tits, as someone yelled.

That same deep-voiced football player got the biggest laughs with one of the nastiest comments of the day.

"Why don't you wear your mom's bra?"

The roars of laughter were thunderously loud. With the whole pavilion now participating – teenagers shouting and the parents silently watching and laughing – he tried to walk faster to get to work while jeers and jibes followed him. At last the concession stand and the public restroom beside it loomed in sight, and he made his final dash to try and escape.

"Fuckin' freak, what are you with those tits?"

"You're disgusting."

"Freak, freak, man why don't you go drown in the lake, no one wants to look at you?"

Asshole, fat pig, nasty pimple face fuck-up with tits; you're disgusting, just kill yourself, do us all a favor so we don't have to look at you.

Those last comments echoed in his ears as he fled into the public restroom. He ran to the bathroom stall at the end and locked himself in, before he dropped down onto the toilet. He rocked back and forth on the toilet seat, looking up at the ceiling. Then he put both hands on his face so he could cry quietly, no one hearing him. He felt the pimples on his face, small pricks of pain, lumpy against his palms, which reminded him what a ravaged disgusting monster his classmates made him out to be.

The door outside opened and he froze, but then he heard men's voices, amplified with echoes from the tiles, talking about women, the game, whatever. He tracked them with his ears, from door to facilities to basin, washing their hands, the blast of the hand dryer, the door being pulled open and swinging shut again on their receding voices.

Wiping away the tears, he tried to gain some composure and straighten himself out to go to work. He opened the door of the bathroom stall and made his way over to the sink – just as the door burst open and four of the teenage classmates from the pavilion came crowding in. He tried to ignore them, though he knew as well as they did that he was trapped, cornered, just like an animal. They blocked him before he could reach the sink.

"Hey, look guys, there's a girl in the men's room!"

He washed his hands as they jostled him, laughing and pushing. They started to poke his soft, titty-like chest, still laughing.

"Hey, he does have tits. What kind of freak of nature are you?"

One of them gave him a shove, another a punch to his stomach and another a hard kick to his ass. Nicholas fell to the floor and they all piled onto him.

He tried to cover his body with his arms and use his hands to cover his face. The door handle rattled. They had locked it, and someone was trying to get in. The rattling changed to a loud knocking. Someone needed to use the place. The teenagers stopped and looked at each other. He stayed down in his curled-up safety position.

"Fuckin' freak!"

They got one last hard kick at him before they pulled the door open and hurried out. They didn't want to be held accountable for their actions. They rushed past the man without stopping, forcing him to step back.

The man stopped in his tracks when he saw him on the floor. Then he ran to help him.

"Are you OK?"

He silently started to get up.

"What happened?"

He did not utter a sound, not one word or any explanation. The man tried to console him as he went to clean his hands at the sink. He splashed water all over his face and tried to make himself presentable for work. As he finished cleaning himself up, he took a quick glance in the mirror. What he saw was a sea of pimples that everyone must endure when looking at him. Without thanking the man, he walked out of the men's room and headed for the concession stand, to work.

*

The man shakes his head in empathy while he goes about his business, thinking about what just happened. He feels bad for the kid, but what could he do? In a few minutes, as always, this whole incident will be a distant memory for all who witnessed it and participated. But Nicholas will not be afforded that indulgence. The luxury of the situation dissipating from memory in a few minutes will never be given to him. That is what happens every time. The memory will stay with Nicholas, stamped into his brain, cataloged in his mind forever.

*

This whole story repeats in my brain as I drive home. After Nicholas told it to me, I couldn't get it into focus. Now I can't shift it.

I get the bedspread in, lay it back out on the bed, decide to take a nap. As usual, Barney joins me. I drop onto the bed and look up at the ceiling, still thinking of what Nicholas had told me. Over and over the words, the sights run through my mind as clearly as if I could see the event. I turn on my side, fix the pillow, trying to find a comfortable position to fall asleep, but I can't. I try to turn completely over to the other side and that doesn't work either. I get up and walk around. The episode that Nicholas shared with me still will not go away.

I go to the refrigerator and start to drink a beer. After an hour there are four empty cans on the table with a fifth in my hand. Loaded up now, I go to bed and crash on my pillow. That does the trick.

I hear the clink of knives and forks and plates, and Amelia, Miranda and Dan talking. I lift my head up and look at the clock. Nighttime. My family are all eating and talking as I stumble my way into the kitchen. Amelia and Dan smile while Miranda looks at her food, ignoring me. I rub my hair.

Amelia asks, "Would you like dinner, honey?"

I stare at her, not knowing what to say. Dan keeps eating. Miranda makes one of her wise ass remarks – "Maybe you would like another beer?" She takes a drink of her water and stares at me with disgust as she sets her glass back on the table.

I slowly turn around to walk back to my bedroom. I stop, turn back around and say, "Fuck off. Everyone. Fuck... off."

I go slowly back to my bedroom, slam the door behind me.

*

The children sat, holding their knives and forks, Daniel's still with a lump of pasta on it, halfway to his mouth. Amelia had never seen them so stunned.

"Okay." She gave them a nervous smile, trying to make light of what had just happened. "So, Dad's still a work in progress. It's early days."

"It will work out," Daniel said slowly, as if he was trying to convince himself he believed it. He finished transporting the pasta to his mouth and chewed slowly.

Amelia loved her son's optimism. He always seemed to believe that, in time, everything worked out. Nothing had changed her own opinion, that her husband, her children's father, should seek psychiatric help.

And Miranda threw the knife and fork down on the plate and pushed her chair back. She was right back to one minute to midnight, this close to disowning her father,

"No. No, no, no, no, no. I'm not having this. No. Fuck us? Fuck you too, Dad!"

She stood up, turned about, marched away. Amelia realized too late where she was going. She leapt up and quickly followed.

"Miranda, wait!"

Miranda didn't wait. She burst into her parents' room, slamming the door against the wall. Her eyes blazed as she approached the bed.

"LISTEN, DADDY!"

He stared up from the bed as she drew in the breath to begin the speech that would destroy him, unman him, shred his nervous system, obliterate every trace of self respect still left in him. The first word was at the back of her mouth, the first of a machine gun volley, ready to launch.

And then she felt Amelia's gentle hands on her shoulders.

"Wait, please, darling, there's so much you don't know."

Miranda turned on mom.

"STOP IT, JUST STOP IT! I am sick of him taking out his frustrations just because he had a bad day."

"Please, Miranda, trust me, there are still things we're not aware of so don't say or do anything, please, my darling, OK?"

Miranda let out a long sigh. Letting her mother win and swallowing her pride.

"That's it. I'm done with him."

Amelia gently guided the fuming Miranda from the room. As they were leaving, a lump rose in her throat as she led Miranda out of the room and gently closed the door.

Miranda wasn't wrong. He had gone too far. And she had no idea what to do. All she knew was that something needed to be done. What?

CHAPTER 15

The clock showed 4:35 a.m. The house was quiet.

There was no point staying in bed. Amelia wouldn't sleep again and the more she searched for the answer, the more it would hide itself. Maybe if she got moving, the answer would make itself known. She might catch a glimpse of it out of the corner of her eye, or maybe it would slide in, trying not to be noticed. She got up quietly, grabbed her robe, and went out.

On the way to the kitchen she passed Daniel's room. The door was open and the room was all lit up. She found him in the kitchen, back at the counter, making himself a snack. A forbidden activity when he was a kid, but he was too old to feel guilty or be told off now. She smiled and said hello but her mind was still on her husband. She sat down, still just looking at nothing.

He came and sat down with his toast. They made small talk but they both had the same things on their minds. Daniel went first.

"So-o-o, is Dad asleep?"

"Yes, he is fast asleep."

"What's with Dad?" Dan burst out. Amelia pulled back slightly. Even calm, placid Dan was reacting now? One more sign of just how bad, how intolerable the situation had grown.

"I mean, all these years he has always been upset, taking things out on us. He yells over the smallest things. We all walk on eggshells when he's around."

"I know, honey, I know. I guess I thought things would get better for him, but things just seem to be getting worse. And I don't know what or how to help him."

"Guess you're talking about Dad, right?"

They looked up. Miranda had come in and she sat down with them. They were each in their usual spots.

There was a moment of silence. Then Amelia said, "Your father has issues from his past and I don't know how to get him help."

More silence. Then they talked, and talked some more between more periods of quiet. Finally, Amelia looked at the clock and she couldn't believe that it showed 7:10 a.m.

"Wow, look at the time! We need to get going."

The kids went quickly to start their morning routines for a normal weekday. Amelia went to her bedroom and found him still asleep. She gazed down at him for a moment. Was there anything she could do right here, right now about this situation?

But she knew it could not be resolved in a few seconds, and right now, she needed to get ready for work. After all, she now was the head of the family. She was the one that supported the others.

*

It is 8:45 a.m. and the three have departed the home. Gone out into the world. Three sound people who have to get out there to support the family. These three are the power dynamos that let this family exist.

Now it's 9:00 a.m. Those three are doing their duty in their own way so that we can all survive.

The clock shows 10:42 a.m. as I raise my head in bed. I have the typical hangover with all its wonderful side effects. I push off the sheets and turn over to put my feet on the floor. My hands are going through my hair as flashbacks enter my mind. Quick, specific and accurate. Thoughts detailing Nicholas's life, of the park incident, of drinking beer, of my conduct affecting the family. But the worst is the memory of telling my family to fuck off. I feel horrible, physically and mentally. Every time this occurs, I know I was wrong. Being intoxicated is not an excuse that holds up well in my heart. I still know I was wrong.

I start my daily routine, with my head ready to explode from the hangover. I drag myself into the kitchen to eat my usual breakfast and then take my medications.

After cleaning up my mess I walk to the bedroom and get into bed again. I pick up my phone and call Amelia. She answers quickly. I don't know if I was lucky enough to get her between calls, or if there's a luckless customer on hold while her failure of a husband tries to make things right.

"Hi honey, how are you?"

She always answers like that, her tone reflecting her smile. It always comes through on the phone and I am always happy to hear it.

"I'm OK. I am sorry how I acted last night. Please could you and the kids..."

She stops me, as usual, to assure me that it's all good. That they have no problems about what happened last night. For the thousandth time. I pause and a moment of silence occurs between us. We both know that it isn't OK but we go along doing as we have always done before, ignoring it and hopefully it will stop. We both know that is not going to happen, but we live the lie once again. My eyes start to brim.

We manage with more small talk, like how we feel physically, what our plans for the day would be, how we will come together for dinner and what we should all eat tonight. Bitter tears are rolling down our faces by now but we keep talking. After all that is said and done, we both say our goodbyes and as we start to hang up, fingers poised to press the appropriate button to end the call, we both close our eyes, trying to stop the flow. Because we both have the same thought – we don't know what steps to take to fix this situation.

*

The day passes as usual for myself, mundane and boring, but I get my assigned chores accomplished. Dinner is waiting for the family to congregate together at our usual time. The four of us sit in our usual seating arrangement and conversation flows normally. It is all general small talk, but we all know we are circling closer and closer to the incident that happened the night before – plus another thousand past examples on our minds.

Miranda is always the one to bring us back to the real world. To ask the question, what the fuck is my problem, and why do they need to suffer? Or some variation on the theme. Left to our own devices, the other three of us could probably skirt around it forever. She sets down her knife and fork, very carefully, on her plate, and I see the movement and I know this is it.

She starts. "Dad, what is going on with you, your life? I know you have health problems, serious ones, and I know what Uncle Tony told us, but why do you get so nasty with us? It's abusive. It ruins all our days, and we all have to deal with it."

At first she is measured and precise, each word carefully placed. It's probably a speech she has prepared during the day, polishing and preparing each word. But as she goes on, the control starts to slip. Her voice grows higher, more strident; the mask slipping from the hurt it is trying to conceal.

"Well, I'm not willing to give you any more passes for this, every time I come home each night. And I know Mom and Dan feel the same. We just don't accept it. We want it to stop!"

Amelia and Dan are slowly moving their food around their plates, looking down, not saying a word, which makes their thoughts clear. They both agree with Miranda.

I look slowly round at each of them, ending with Miranda. She is staring directly at me with her beautiful, emerald green eyes. Those eyes, which I cherish in my heart, show how she feels in her own heart. She is disgusted with me, and her eyes show she means it. They say it will not be tolerated anymore.

I don't know what to say to my family. How can I answer her questions or her demands if I don't know what to do? I look down, then up again. There is dead silence.

"How do you feel? Guys?" Looking first at Amelia, then Daniel. It's a stupid question, just buying time, because I know all too well they agree with Miranda. They don't even bother to answer.

I say, "I am sorry, I don't know, I don't know, I don't know what to do."

All three of them have their eyes on me now. But how can I start to explain something I don't understand myself? I know they are right, but what to do? – I have no clue.

Daniel offers his opinion to the room at large. He can't bear to talk directly to me.

"Maybe Dad should see a counselor?"

I flinch at the word. I've always hated it. *Counseling*. Some busybody know-nothing outsider sticking their nose into my business, telling me what to do. My problems are my family's problems, no one else's.

But maybe we could all face it together. A united front. I look at him. "Like family counseling?"

Miranda shoots up, her chair flying backwards.

"No, you need counseling! You need help, not us. You're the one who's been messing up our home for years now. We were just kids, then we were teenagers, but we are adults now, so we do not need to take this shit from you anymore. We three are sick of tiptoeing around you every second of the day. When I get calls from you... Dad, when was the last time you talked to me on the phone?"

I'm puzzled. I can't see what it has to do with anything. But she has the floor and I try to think.

"I... don't know," I say. "I mean, I try, from time to time, but I generally get voicemail..."

"You *always* get voicemail, Dad, because I've set my phone

that way! Because I can't bear to talk to you! Because I have zero feelings of caring, I just don't care what you want or what you're after. Do you get that? I see your number on my cell phone, and I get disgusted, and then I get afraid you might just be going to yell a load of shit at me. So I let voicemail take it. I don't want to speak with you!"

Amelia now protests. "Miranda, that's really very hard on your father."

Miranda answers, "No, Mom, I don't care. I want him to know how I feel inside, and I think you both should tell him too about how you feel. I know you feel the same but you're too afraid to tell him. Well, I'm not. Do you get it, Dad? We are sick of living in the same house with you and we are just plain sick of you, period! Do you get it?!"

Miranda pushes her plate forward and storms to her bedroom. The door slam shakes the house. Dan and Amelia stare at each other, not knowing what to say. Not even a one-word answer. I look at them both. I push my seat slowly back and walk to my bedroom and slowly close the door.

*

It was like the end of the world just happened in their little home, like a bomb was dropped on top of their house, and Amelia and Dan just sat there in the midst of the debris. The explosion happened with a cloud of smoke and fire that obscured everything, and as the smoke slowly cleared they could see the destruction left behind.

The usual thoughts came to mind. How to clean up the mess caused by the bomb? But no one knew what to do to end the war. No one knew how to pick up the pieces of their destroyed world.

*

I hear Amelia and Dan cleaning. Thirty minutes pass before Amelia comes in and gently closes the door. She smiles as usual, trying to comfort me.

"You know your daughter. She's just like you, always dramatic." Amelia laughs but it's an uncomfortable laugh. For all her other amazing abilities, she is not a good actor.

"Just like me? I hope not," I say. I stand up and face her. "She sees my number on her cell and gets disgusted that I am calling her? I make my own daughter look at numbers and she is disgusted?"

My voice catches in my throat. For all the days of my life that I suffered, nothing compares to what Miranda said to me today, and I don't blame her. I'm blaming myself.

"Do you know what stupid thing came to my mind when she left the room? I was thinking that if she feels that way just looking at numbers then she will never have pictures of me in her office or in her home. Isn't that crazy, to think my daughter won't display a picture of her own father? In fact, there's nothing she won't do to cut me out of her life. My God, Amelia!"

I fall to my knees, sobbing uncontrollably, banging my fists on the floor.

CHAPTER 16

Nothing else can be said except that we all go back to our lives. The problem that plagues our family is finally diagnosed but we are all lost as to how to find a cure. So, we all go back to playing our characters as if we were all in a movie. The role we play each day, with all rehearsals completed years ago as we know the script by heart. We do the narrative of our characters perfectly now. An Academy Award performance by us all. How sad it is to see this continue. So unfair for my family.

*

I get our laundry load for the week on laundry day. Everyone has their loads ready for me. As I park the car and gather everything up, I see Nicholas enter the laundromat ahead of me. I lock up and go in after him. As usual, Bertha smokes her brains out while folding clothing into its assigned plastic clear bags next to a big sign that reads NO SMOKING. I chuckle as I walk past.

"Hello, Bertha."

She answers back, of course with a cigarette dangling from her lips, "Hi, Mac, how have you been?" I stop and we get into a small conversation. If you could call our exchange a conversation. It always feels to me that we exchange words, but

Bertha does not pay attention.

Today I will finally learn that this is not true. She is an abrupt, pushy woman but deep down I know she is a kindhearted soul. And she does listen to every word. I will learn this – just not yet.

Suddenly, a big comforter comes flying at me, making me drop my own things as I try to grab hold of it. I keep hold of it and help her fold it. It is the last item for the plastic customer pick-up bag. She thanks me, smiles, and hands me some free coins to use today for my load. I thank her and she says, "You're welcome." She blows smoke in my face and goes back to her office.

I gather my stuff and stand in the doorway as she makes herself comfortable in a chair.

"So, Bertha, how's your sister?"

She blows another large amount of smoke in my direction.

"She's fine. She can be a pain in my neck but she's my best friend, you know."

She continues, "I hate her because she always did what she wanted to do, never following directions. You know, that bugs the hell out of me." As she says it, she is stubbing out her cigarette into a full ash tray and blowing out her last breath of smoke.

I say, "Wow, the nerve! I wonder where she learned her ways?"

Bertha knows exactly what I am trying to say.

"Hmm! How was your week?"

I tell her what I always say to people who ask me that question. That I had a nice week. I know that is not the case and so does the person talking to me, but it is part of my role in this movie, this movie my family and I play in together.

We stand there in that position doing our usual banter. I look over to my favorite corner and see Nicholas sitting waiting for me. I tell Bertha I need to get my things done. Bertha watches me intently as I get my load into the washer and make myself comfortable in my favorite chair. The machine spins into action and I can begin speaking to Nicholas.

"How are you, Nicholas. Did you have a good week?"

Yes, I ask him the same question other people ask me, and his answer might be just as truthful. As usual, he doesn't look up. Maybe it saves him the trouble of pretending.

"Nothing's changed."

A pause.

"Nothing changes."

I open my mouth and he gets there first.

"Except that things get worse. That's the only kind of change in my life."

His eyes. So lonely. No one's life should be that empty.

"Is there anyone at school you can talk to?" I ask. As soon as I start flapping my mouth, I can sense where this might go but for some perverse reason I have to keep going. I'm a grown-up, in front of a kid. We're meant to be the ones in charge, the ones who can help and protect the little one. "Any... friend...?"

To my surprise, he does answer.

"There was this boy..." He trails off. I'm on the verging of trying to encourage him to go on when he does so anyway.

"I was off sick. Bad sick. I spent some weeks in hospital. You know what's funny, I thought the kids in school would have some empathy or anything that I was seriously sick." He looks up at me, straight in the eyes, out of those twin pits of loneliness. "They couldn't care less. I heard that every time I missed school, there was this one kid who would say, 'He's out again, must be doing a sex change operation.' That got big laughs, my one friend said to me. He was picked on so much more because he was Jewish and that made him one step even below me."

I close my eyes. It's bad but it doesn't trigger me like his other stories have. Maybe because it's longer ago, maybe because his voice is quiet and level as he says it – conversational, if you can call it conversational when all emotion and feeling and nuance is drained out of it. This kind of stuff is just baseline for him. Another normal, fucked-up day in our normal, fucked-up world.

But I think I see a ray of hope.

"So this other kid, this Jewish friend...?"

A simple shake of the head tells me the kid is not on the scene anymore. Maybe he was scared off. Maybe he shifted schools. Maybe he turned his shirt and joined in the persecution. Whatever, he is no longer a friend of Nicholas.

I look away. My cell phone alarm goes off and I stand.

"I need to take a certain medication," I say. I point at the chair where he's sitting. "You wait there, right?"

He makes a move that isn't a nod or a head shake. I get the pill from its box in my laundry bag and head to the back room where there is a water fountain.

*

Bertha had been thinking for a long time and she had decided the day had finally come. She saw it coming the very first time she met him running back to the laundromat. She was just waiting for the right moment. It had finally arrived.

She pulled a bit of paper towards her and started to write.

*

I take a sip of water and swallow the pill.

I stare blankly at the wall, my mind full of the lonely, hurting boy behind me. Daniel teaches kids that sort of age. What would Daniel say to him?

It's more than a rhetorical question, because of course I know the answer. Daniel would say to him what he said to me. Get help. See a counselor. And to my surprise, it suddenly sounds not such a bad idea. Not when I'm passing it on to someone else.

So I wipe my mouth with my hand and go back to the dryer where my clothes are all done. Bertha is at the front, with that cigarette dangling from her mouth, neatly putting away my things. I look around for Nicholas and he is gone.

As I look around some more, suddenly Bertha is standing right in front of me, and I recoil slightly, because there's a look on her face that I've never seen before.

CHAPTER 17

I am at home, putting my things away. All the clothing is in its right place, the soaps and dryer sheets are too, and my personal belongings, like my medications, are organized. I take a seat, reach into my pocket, and pull out the paper Bertha gave me.

"Hey, Mac, give this guy a call. I know him well and I bet you will know him well too. He is someone in my life that if I am correct is someone you want in your life."

She blows smoke in my face and walks away. I cough a little, gather up my belongings and make my way out. I pause at the door to her office and am about to say something, but she interrupts me.

"Look, Mac. You've been coming here for a while. I see you and I see myself years ago. Just call this number, I think it will help you as it did for me. Get it, Mac?"

That damn smoke goes into my face. I wave it away, coughing. She smiles and tells me, *"See you next week."* She turns away to finish her cigarette. I give a small smile and walk with my things to my car.

I must be staring at it for an eternity. It may just be a minute, but that's how I feel. And instead I call Amelia's cell. She answers as always. Positive, loving; you can feel her smile through the warmth of her tone.

"So, honey..." I can already sense the workload piling up while she allows herself the luxury of talking to me.

"Are you busy, honey?"

I know, I'm just making her busier by asking questions like that instead of just getting to the point.

"Well, yes, but I can..."

"I'm going to get help," I blurt out. Silence. "You know. Get therapy. I... I feel it may help our family's situation." Still silence. "*My* situation, I mean. And then the family's. So, um, so, I'm going to see someone."

I imagine her closing her eyes. She can't believe what I am saying. She is happy that I have finally come to this conclusion. She isn't the type to say, "I told you so," but she always has the right to. She just never says those words.

We speak some more, but I know she really needs to get back to work, and I'm fighting back tears, and I think she might be too.

"Sweet pea, I am sorry it took me so long to get to this point in my life."

I can sense that Amelia's eyes are still closed at the other end of the line. She is wiping away her tears, never letting me know she, too, is crying. She answers, "It's fine. I am glad you realize what you need to do, that you know now it's never too late to help yourself. Finding this person to help is a great step forward. But... honey, what changed?"

I could tell her, *the manager at the laundromat gave me this number*, which would be one hundred percent true but not really helpful. She knows who Bertha is but suddenly it doesn't sound like that compelling a reason.

"Oh, just thinking about it," I say.

There is complete silence on the line. We both try so hard not to let each other know how upset we are. But even though we are upset, this time we are happy because now we both know maybe things will become better for me and for our family.

"I love you, sweetheart. Always did, always will, no matter."

Amelia replies, "I know, honey. I think this is great. Let's talk some more later tonight. OK?"

I answer, "Sure. I love you, Amelia."

She replies, "I love you too, Nicholas."

Nicholas? No one has called me that since I was a kid.

CHAPTER 18

I stare at Bertha's piece of paper. It has a name and a phone number. I call the number from my cell. It starts to ring. Two rings. On the third ring, I hang up. I get up, go to get a beer, and sit back down. I press memory, and it redials. Third ring, then a fourth ring. I hang up again. I can't do it. I get up, walk to the garbage, throw away the paper, and go to my bedroom for my day's nap. I'm asleep in a minute.

*

We are all at dinner, and as usual, Miranda and I do all the talking while Amelia and Dan just give one-word answers. Things settle down. This is the way things go with us four. We all have our part. We are on the peace-time narrative until I go into another episode. Usually, it takes weeks of peace, and then a war breaks out. Now that the kids are older, especially Miranda, they're not going to take the crap I spout out of my mouth anymore. They aren't little ones that I can bully. They know this, Amelia knew this a long time ago, and I am finally getting it into my head too.

I haven't told anyone about intending to make that call... apart from Amelia. And she says nothing because she knows it's my story to tell, when I'm ready. But the occasional sideways glance, the expectant hesitation when she opens her mouth as if she might be about to interrupt something important from me – I can tell she's dying to know.

If the kids sense something's up, they hide it well. Unfortunately I have given them a lifetime's practice of hiding stuff. They're good at it, all for the wrong reasons.

It's about 11 p.m. and we are all in our accustomed places. Dan is in his room doing his own thing, usually until 4 a.m. Miranda has been fast asleep since 9:45 p.m. Amelia is watching TV in bed as I listen, with ear headphones, to white noise to drown out the TV shows. The house is set with all of us doing our own things, weekday bedtime rituals.

I clear my throat.

"That thing..."

Immediately she's all ears.

"Yes?"

"I have decided not to go seek help."

I see the tiniest flash of disappointment, before her usual calm reasserts itself. She's also had way too much practice at hiding her feelings when her husband lets her down again, and I can't stand it. "It didn't work out. But I'll keep looking."

I can feel the unspoken questions in her eyes, boring into my back, as I determinedly turn over and go to sleep.

*

I wake up at my usual time. Always 9:15 a.m. I don't know why, but I just do it, and it's always around that time. Always! I get up, go into my morning routine. I check the kitchen, make all the beds in the house, and check the bathrooms to make sure they are all up to par. I love my family, but I live with the Three Little Pigs.

Funny, I never thought about that nursery tale until this second. I'm just leaving the last bathroom, my last check of the day, thinking of that rhyme and saying to myself, "Three little pigs, and I guess that makes me the bad old wolf who has come to blow this house down." I smile, thinking about that, when suddenly my cell phone rings. Local code. It's that number I called yesterday.

I look left and right, wondering what to do. After the fourth ring, it goes to voicemail.

I'm happy I changed my mind. I don't want to speak to him anymore. Sure, I told Amelia that I was looking into finding a therapist, but I planned to just let it go, hoping it all goes away. I mean, look at last night. Our dinner together. We were all happy. Things are great. I don't need help.

I put my phone on the counter and I walk away, happy it stopped ringing. It starts again. I stop in my tracks, slowly make my way back. I see that number again. No name, but it's still that number. The number Bertha gave me. I approach slowly, looking at it, wishing it would stop. Wishing this person would leave me alone. On the fourth ring, it stops again. I stare at the phone, happy the person has gone away. I turn to go into the den to watch some TV. As I'm walking away, I don't hear a ring. It's much worse. It's that sound your cell makes when it receives a voicemail. I stop in my tracks again. I turn slowly and walk back to the counter. You'd think that my cell phone was a vicious dog, the way I'm acting. I check the screen and I see one voicemail registered. I decide to listen to it. I mean, I could, right? No harm in listening. I dial into my voicemail and play the message.

"*Hi, I received a call from this number yesterday. The person called and...*" The man stops for a few seconds, then starts again, talking. "*Look, if you're looking for me, I will be glad to talk to you. If you need my assistance, or any type of service, please call back? My name is Doctor Silverman. Thank you, and have a nice day.*"

I stare at the phone while I go to the den sofa to sit and watch TV. I play the message back four times. I decide to erase it and not call back, but as I watch the TV the message keeps playing in my head. This TV show is on for seventeen minutes, but if someone asks me what it is all about, I wouldn't be able to answer.

I mute the TV sound. Staring at the cell, I feel my heart racing. What to do? I look at the TV and then down at my cell. I press the button to redial the number. As I put the phone to my ear, my hand trembles.

The doctor answers on my third ring.

"*Hello?*"

I don't even open my mouth. Just listen. That voice belongs to someone who could change my life. Or fuck it up for ever more.

"*Hello, is anyone there?*" I'm silent, about to hang up the phone when the doctor asks, "*Hello, is this the person who called me yesterday?*" I say nothing. He continues, "*Listen, I'm Doctor Silverman. Please tell me your name. May I be of any assistance?*"

I have no intention of speaking but for some reason my mouth decides now would be a good time to start making sounds. I'm as surprised as anyone.

"I, um, yes, I called yesterday, sir, um, a friend of mine, her name is Bertha." I just realized I don't know Bertha's last name. "Yes, my friend's name is Bertha. Do you know her?"

The doctor answers, "*Bertha Hamilton?*"

I tell him the truth. "I don't know her last name. She manages a laundromat."

The doctor answers, "*Yes, that is Bertha Hamilton. How may I help you?*"

This must be how a bug feels when you lift up the rock. Scared, exposed, nervous. Every scrap of cover whisked away out of reach. Someone I don't even know wants to invade my little world. That world is closed off. Dead. I want it to stay dead. I mean, when something dies, you bury it, right? We are silent for at least fifteen seconds. For me, once again, time seems like an eternity. The doctor starts again.

"*Hi, what is your name?*"

He's unburying the dead.

I answer, "Ah, um, well, ah, um, Nicholas."

He answers, "*Hello, Nicholas. Very nice to meet you. Look, I see you're apprehensive. It's fine. I've come across this many, many times. Bertha, she's a character, right?*"

He likes Bertha and Bertha likes him. That's two big ticks in his favor. I laugh and say, "She is that."

Now we both laugh, and he continues.

"*Why don't you just come in one day and meet? We can talk more in person and take it from there. You can always cancel. I promise you, if we make an appointment and you decide to cancel, I promise not to call back. Okay?*"

He's not holding me to anything. He's putting the rock

back. In my mind, I think that's a great idea. We talk some more. I start to feel more comfortable. This is all new to me. I was raised to believe that you don't need help with your mental health. It shows weakness and it is silly to get this kind of medical treatment. These are the beliefs that have plagued me all these years. I don't tell the doctor about them.

Anyway, we make an appointment for this coming Friday at 1 p.m. We say a few more things to each other. He repeats the thing about canceling and pledges an oath not to call me back. His pledge and voice are very sincere. I feel comfortable with his phone demeanor. He gives me the address – it's on Northern Boulevard and I realize I know it by sight. I've driven past it who knows how many times. He repeats the day and time, and politely hangs up the phone. But first he says one last thing that makes me more comfortable with him.

"You have taken the first steps. And that's a great thing. Have a nice day."

I hang up and stare at the TV show I was watching. I'm not thinking about the doctor's message anymore. I watched the rest of the show. Back to my world. I call Amelia at noon. The TV show is over. I tell her about Doctor Silverman over on Northern Boulevard. She's happy I did this thing.

"And, we won't say anything to the kids until after this first appointment, right?"

"Right."

I know I can trust Amelia with any news. Her mind is a steel trap. She never talks about anything or anyone's private things. She never gossips. She never has negative things to say. She is a true person and will always put the best interests of our family first. But most of all, she respects people's privacy.

She'll even respect my choice if I change my mind again. Friday is days away.

CHAPTER 19

Friday arrives, and I am supposed to see Doctor Silverman today. Waking up does not fill me with joy.

I do my normal routines around the house. The morning routine helps me forget about my appointment at 1 p.m. Every time I think about it, I get nervous, scared. The rock starts to lift up again. I just want to forget the idea of seeing Doctor Silverman. Every minute of the morning, I keep giving myself reasons in my head to avoid going. I start adding new chores to my routine just to make myself late. All routines for the day are accomplished. I look at the clock and see it is 10:45 a.m.

Now what? I know I am doomed. I have to get ready.

Look, I tell myself, are you like this when you go to see a regular doctor? Of course not. I have to take care of my health.

So I tell myself to surrender. I push aside all those thoughts telling me not to go and decide to think of this appointment as a regular medical check-up.

It helps, a little.

I get out of the shower and wonder what to wear. I have no idea. What does one wear to see this kind of physician? My mind fills with stereotypes. I picture a big sofa with an ugly old man, with a long yellow pad, sitting next to me in a chair. Can you believe it? I shake my head and try to think better of the situation. I decide to relax. I put on a clean pair of jeans and a comfortable pullover. I figure we'll talk for an hour, so I wear something very comfortable. I grab my pants, and as I put them on, I smell the laundromat. I smile, laugh to myself, thinking of Bertha. Trust me, she is a sight to see and hear.

I get dressed, put on my baseball cap, grab my car keys. I look back at the kitchen to make sure the oven, stove and toaster are all off. I'm nuts about the house catching fire. I always double-check those three things before I leave. I make sure Barney is okay, too. Settled, and with water in his bowl.

I'm sending out the wrong signals. One of us is getting ready to go out, so he thinks it's his time for his walk.

"No, Barney, I'm going out to an appointment. We can go out later when I get home." I swear, he understands English. He stops being a happy little Maltese, walks back to his rest spot, and lies down. I look at him and say, "I promise, when I return, we'll go for our walk."

I grab the door handle and take one last look back at him. I truly believe this dog understands. I smile at him. He is lying down fully, his body level with the floor, his head between his paws and his tail waving up and down in a happy goodbye. I continue on my journey.

*

I think of the hill on Northern Boulevard as Doctor's Row, because there are rows of buildings going on for about four miles, all with different kinds of doctors in them. I pull up to one of the nicer offices in this row. The building is beautiful – tall, majestic, and made entirely of black glass, so you can't look inside, but the people inside can look out.

The parking lot is large with plenty of options. Usually, at this time of day, handicap parking is available, so I use a space. I take my trustworthy handicap ID from my glove compartment and hang it on the rear-view mirror. I sit there, looking at the time. I'm five minutes early, as usual. I tap the steering wheel, looking side to side. I see people going in and out of the building. Tap, tap, tap. I just keep tapping the wheel, thinking I should make a run for it. I close my eyes, take a deep breath, and get out of the car.

I begin to breathe deeply as I walk towards the entrance. I'm getting nervous, very nervous. I press the key to lock the car. The sound of the car locking fills my ears, and I hear nothing else. The sounds of traffic, cars, buses, people are all around me, yet I hear none of them. I locked myself out of my escape route. I have no choice but to go forward.

*

"Excuse me, sir?"

I hear him as I walk inside. A guy in a suit and tie, quiet and discreet, standing politely over to one side by a pedestal like a lectern.

I turn and say, "Yes?" and the whole world rushes back into my ears. I no longer have that blast of silence. People think silence has no sound, but to me, it is deafening. That silence is worse than loud noises because it makes you feel invisible.

"Sir, are you all right?"

I answer, "Um, yes, I have an appointment with Doctor Silverman."

"Yes, sir." He holds out an arm, pointing across the lobby. "Just straight ahead and to your right."

I thank him and head that way. The lobby is three or four floors high with glass-walled balconies on every side. So much commotion, all around me. People walking this way and that, women looking in their handbags, people on their phones, people in wheelchairs being pushed to their destinations. There are four large elevators at the center of the building. All the people in them can see out into the lobby as they go up and down. It's a world inside a world, I think. The building is truly majestic, and I lose myself in marveling at it until I see the door to my destination.

*

I stop in front of the door. It's plain, just a tasteful little plaque with Doctor Silverman's name on it, and a few initials for his qualifications. I hesitate, thinking, wanting to turn and leave. I know that by walking into this office, my life will change forever. Whether for good or bad, I don't know. All I know is that by turning this handle, my life will be different from this day forward. It will be a new life for me and my family.

I reach for the handle and then I turn the motion into raising my hand to knock. But my knuckles don't make contact with the wood. Not yet.

Only Amelia knows I'm here, and she doesn't even really know that much. I could still just as well be at home. And the kids know nothing. If I walked away, she would understand and they would never know.

But if they *did* know, if they somehow found out... And it's thinking of the kids that does it. In fact it's thoughts of what Miranda said that hit me like a prizefighter's punches. The knockout blow is what she said about seeing my number on her phone. That she doesn't care and sends it to voicemail. And with that thought, I turn the handle.

CHAPTER 20

You know, it's funny the difference between what you think you know and what you see. I remember my ideas of what Doctor Silverman might look like – some cliched cartoon Freud lookalike, with a big yellow legal pad, wanting to know about my childhood.

Doctor Silverman's office reception waiting area – as stated on a sign on the wall – is immaculate and beautiful, but not like some show home where you don't dare touch anything in case you spoil it. It's decorated in a way that makes a person feel relaxed and comfortable. A pot of reed diffusers lends a gentle, not over-stated scent to the atmosphere. A fireplace that works is crackling softly in the wall. I bend down to look, and it is a real fireplace.

I walk around, studying the beautiful art on the walls and an enormous library of books. This guy is either the real thing or a real phony. A fine-looking wooden desk has a sign telling his patients to wait and make themselves comfortable, or get a bottled water or a cup of coffee. So that's what I do. I grab a bottle of water, which is five dollars retail, and sit down on the leather sofa. It creaks beneath me as it absorbs my weight.

My eyes continue to wander admiringly around the room, and they come across the door. I stop and stare at it. That is where he will appear. The man who will shake my life from top to bottom. Who will ask me all those questions I don't want to answer. Who will interfere with what little equilibrium I have, set me adrift on an ocean where I have no idea what will happen next.

That little voice comes in my head again. "OK, just get up and leave."

I brace my hands on the sofa, leaning forward, halfway to getting up.

"Hello, are you Mr. Rato? Very nice to meet you. I am Doctor Silverman."

He has appeared from another door, one I hadn't noticed before. A very handsome, distinguished man in a Brooks Brothers suit.

I get up, look at the door I came through, and say, "I changed my mind, thank you."

I start to gather my things together and he doesn't move to stop me, which is disconcerting. Just stands and looks. I can tell from his body language that it's not even like he's struck dumb by my actions. His silence is intentional. He's just letting me do it. I'm not used to getting zero push-back, not even an expression or a roll of the eyes to say what the other person really thinks.

But he does tell me, "Mr. Rato, wait. I am not going to force you. I would like you to decide to stay on your own. You're here; let us just talk. You took a big step forward just arriving here."

I look down at the floor, shaking my head side to side. I say, "I thought I was ready for this, but I don't know, Doctor,

I just don't know."

We stand there for what seems to be forever. It is probably a few seconds. Doctor Silverman says, "Let's go inside my office and just sit for a while."

I ask, "You're friends with Bertha and she comes here?"

He begins to laugh and says, "I know what you mean, and if you know her well enough for her to refer you here, then you must know she is truly a good person inside. Yes, my patients are usually celebrities, politicians, the more affluent, but I'm happy to help anyone who wants my services. I was getting divorced and I did some laundry there; well, you really can't miss someone like her, and she is a lovely lady at heart. But enough of Bertha, I'm glad you came in."

We both give each other a small grin. In an odd way, our conversation about Bertha helps me relax. I take a long sigh and walk into his office. I enter first. I hear him walk in behind me and close the door.

*

His office is just as impeccably decorated, tasteful with a calming affectation. Same sort of decor and scents, and there's something else I can't quite identify. I look around, trying to see where I should sit. And yes, there's a sofa over to one side. I was right about that, at least. But he directs me to a chair in front of his desk and walks around to sit opposite me.

"You have a nice office," I state. He smiles.

"Thank you."

We sit there, just staring at each other. I look at him, then look away. This pattern of behavior continues for about a minute. I just don't know how to start, what to say, where to begin. So, I say as much, out loud.

"Doctor, I don't know how to start, what to say, where to begin."

And the words keep coming out of my mouth. "I don't know, I don't know…"

Usually, when a person says those words, they *do* know. They do have something to say. It is just easier, safer to say, "I don't know," over and over. But in this case it's true.

"What do you want me to say, Doctor?" I say out loud. My smile is gone now, and I am being more aggressive. I am becoming more confident, I guess. Surer that I want to leave. I say, "How does this work? Do I start saying how bad my childhood was, that I come from a broken home, my dad beat me and my mother?"

Doctor Silverman says, "Why don't you just say hello?"

I sit up straight in my chair, look right into him, and say, "Hello. Am I all cured now?"

He sits back and looks at me and says, "Hello, very pleased to meet you. I am glad you came today. Let me try and explain certain ground rules. This process will work only if you want to be here. I am not here to say that I will cure you of your situation or even change it. At this point in time, at your age, change cannot occur. I am here to help you understand that these sessions will help you become aware of your behaviors. Help you recognize and adjust an old behavior into a new way to have a peaceful atmosphere with your family, friends, coworkers, and most of all with yourself. These sessions will empower you to take control of your feelings, which create your behaviors. These sessions will help you adjust your behavior to more appropriate solutions to live your life in a better manner. Please understand that I will never promise you that you will change. If you believe that after a certain time, you and your life will change, then I ask you to leave now. I can guarantee that will never happen with any session, here or with another doctor. But I can also guarantee that I can help you realize these concepts and help you to react better in situations, which will lead to a happy life."

I sit back, my mouth maybe hanging open a little. That was a lot of words but what I picked up on was, this guy will be charging me out of my medical pension with no guarantee of making me better.

No, scratch that. I'm pretty sure he specifically said he *can't* make me better.

Two things keep me in my place, and one is that my family wants me to be here so I should at least make a try of it. And the other is that he used the word "help". Even if it's not the help I was after, it's help of a kind. More help than I've ever had from any other direction.

So while I digest his little speech, I keep on looking around, and I realize I've worked out that extra something I noticed when I came in. There's a little machine on his desk, very quietly making wave noises. The magic box has all the white sounds of the day. I like it.

He sees the direction I'm looking in.

"I prefer not to watch the time. It's a distraction to me and to my clients. The noises give me signals about where we are at in time. Is it OK? Would you like another sound?"

"It's fine," I tell him sincerely. The white noise is a link with the laundromat. It defines Doctor Silverman's office as a safe space.

He smiles and leans forward, chin propped on his two fingers.

"Well, here is how I think we should proceed. Today's appointment is at no charge. I've already given you a lot to think about, and maybe some preconceptions to process. We'll start getting down to business next time and I'd like that to be... tomorrow?" He swivels his laptop – thin and minimalist – around to run his eyes over the screen. "I have another client coming in at 10 a.m., so you would be welcome at 11:15 a.m."

"That's a Saturday," I point out.

"Would that be a problem?"

I realize that, no, it isn't, really. Saturdays, weekends, are different for my family with their Monday to Friday workloads. For me, one day is pretty much like another.

"No problem," I say. He nods, and smiles.

"Good. Tomorrow we will talk some more, and based on what transpires from that I will make my recommendation for how, when and how often we should continue to meet."

"You don't think you'll make me better tomorrow?" I joke. Fortunately he sees it as what it is. He doesn't repeat his little talk about not actually curing me.

"With your permission, I'll just make some notes now."

He smiles and takes out a leather-bound, lined yellow pad. I burst out laughing.

"Ah! You know, I thought about this ugly old man in a bad suit in a cheap office with a couch with a pad like that, and him sitting next to me while I lie on his couch. That's sick, right? My preconceived thoughts."

Doctor Silverman laughs.

"Well, first, let me say it is OK to have any thoughts you like, if you correct them and learn from the experience. This is a perfect example of what I meant before. You see how you thought about something and how your answer reflected those thoughts. I will help you understand how preconceptions like that come to mind. They do to all of us as human beings. You will learn to take notice of that mentally and learn how to better answer your preconceived thoughts, learn to live a better life when you're subjected to uncomfortable thoughts and situations. Usually, our past experiences dictate our way of handling situations in our lives in the present as well as the future."

I start to feel comfortable, and now Bertha, with the cigarette hanging out of her mouth, is pictured in my head. I understand why she thought he would be a good person to talk to too. He continues to explain to me how the process works.

"There are no wrong answers – except for any untruthful ones. They are wrong. You need to be completely, one hundred percent truthful in all your answers, all your responses to my questions. And everything you say is protected under state and federal law. Only if a crime is being committed can your documents be unsealed, and even then, only first to a judge, who would read your files privately to see if there is any relevant information."

"I've got nothing illegal to confess," I say, and it's good to be able to say it with complete confidence. There's so much other crap, so much I have got wrong, so much harm I have caused, but on that count I am genuinely blameless.

He smiles. "It's all so many details. I just want to reassure you that whatever you say will always be private and not accessible. Now, I'm afraid your time is up for today."

I look at my watch, and he's right. The wave machine must have sent him some coded signal only he understands.

"So, do you want to make that appointment for tomorrow?"

I don't hesitate, but at the same time I suddenly can't say a simple word like, "Yes," out loud. So, I nod and make an affirmative sort of *uh-huh* grunt. He bows his head and taps quickly at the computer. There, I'm in. It's official.

I stand up to go, and head for the door I came in by.

"Ah, not that one!" He's standing, too, smiling. He gestures a hand at a second door. "I ask my clients to go out that way. It keeps it private – that way they won't cross each other."

For some reason, that's what impresses me the most about this doctor's office. I nod, and go out the approved way.

*

As I drive home I am thinking of the office building, the parking lot, his beautiful office, and the doctor's words about not changing but adjusting. I get home, and as I step into the kitchen, Barney is waiting, tongue lolling and tail wagging hard enough to fight the ceiling fans. I crouch down to pet him.

"You're always here! No matter how I act or feel, you always love to see me."

Barney runs around in a circle out of sheer joy that I am home. Barney always lifts my spirits, makes my day brighter no matter what mood I am feeling. He is always helpful in that I forget all my problems in my head.

I hope that Doctor Silverman somehow will find the same recipe that Barney uses on me. If only Doctor Silverman can accomplish that feat. If only.

CHAPTER 21

Saturday mornings are a dead zone in our home. I have to say I am a very lucky man. My wife, son, and daughter are truly committed to their work life. Mondays to Fridays, they give one hundred and ten percent effort every time they go to work. So, when they have time allotted for taking off, they take full advantage. Saturday mornings, my family are justifiably in their beds, enjoying every moment of sleeping in as long as possible.

Barney, well, he just sleeps all the time. As Amelia says many times, "He works so hard being cute, he gets exhausted."

I come out of the shower and look at my wife sleeping with Barney at her feet. It makes me crack a smile while I get dressed for Doctor Silverman's appointment at 11:15. Barney picks his little head up as he watches me intently, wondering where I am going. I slowly leave my room. Just as I am about to close the door gently, I hear my wife speak quietly.

"So, you going to see him today? You decided to start this process?"

I stop, turn around.

"Yes, I think the time has arrived."

Amelia raises her head and touches Barney, a gentle pat on his back as he too lifts himself up on the bed. She positions herself better for speaking, propping herself up on one elbow.

"You're doing the right thing, Nick, I really believe that." Barney starts to wag his tail. "You see, Barney agrees with me too." One of her big, award-winning smiles flashes on her face.

I return a quick, nervous smile. "Thanks, you two. I love you both. I'll call you driving home, sweet pea."

I pass Dan's room, and even with his door closed, I still hear his snoring. It sounds like a big moose call from the woods. I shake my head, laughing at myself. I feel sorry for whoever must deal with that in his future.

My daughter's bedroom door is closed. As I pass her room, I think how sorry I am and hope we can fix our relationship.

*

I love the traffic on Saturday mornings in Manhasset, New York. There isn't any. The streets are empty. I am driving my white Lexus, enjoying my favorite tunes on my CD player. And I am thinking about what is going to happen soon.

That's just the thing – I have no idea what to expect. Maybe that is a good thing. I decide to just do this second visit and follow his number one rule: to be completely one hundred per cent honest, no holdbacks, no lies of omission, just be completely transparent. That is the plan here. I am going to do this right from the start.

*

The parking lot is almost completely empty except for a few cars. I guess other doctors or businessmen in this building have Saturday hours as well. I lock my car and walk in. That same doorman greets me. He smiles and bids me a good morning, and I in turn do the same. I continue to Doctor Silverman's office, straight back and to the right. Once again, I stop, take a deep breath, sigh, turn the door handle, and walk in.

The time is 10:55 a.m., so I get a cup of coffee while making myself comfortable in one of the chairs by the fireplace. I sit there sipping my coffee while I look at the fireplace. I am thinking how nice this must feel in the dead of winter. I hear a door open. I don't even realize that the time is now 11:10 a.m.. I hear my name.

"Mr. Rato, would you like to come in?"

It hits me at that very moment that this is really happening. I get up with my coffee and make my way into his office.

*

Once again, he asks me to have a seat. I say, "So, there's no sofa that I lie down on while you sit next to me with your yellow pad. Right?"

He smiles. "As you see, I do have a sofa. I want you to be as comfortable as possible so please, pick either a chair or the sofa."

I take the same chair as I did yesterday. He makes his way around to the other side of his desk and we sit, looking at each other. I glance side to side sometimes, and he follows my face with his eyes, never taking them off me.

I have a feeling that if I waited for him to start things going, I could wait forever. It's up to me.

"I don't know what to do?"

Doctor Silverman says, "OK, let me help you here. Why

don't you start by telling me why you are here seeking therapy and what you plan to accomplish on these visits? Just relax, be totally truthful, and take your time. Come to terms with what results you're hoping to gain."

I look down at my feet, take a deep breath, and start.

"Doctor, I want to have a better relationship with my family, especially with my daughter, and with myself. My daughter believes me to be an abusive father, and my son and wife silently agree."

He isn't shocked. No judgment, not even an acknowledgment I've said something significant.

Doctor Silverman says, "Well, can you tell me why they feel you're abusive? Share a situation with me and let us start from that point."

Memories flash suddenly in front of my eyes. The laundromat, that kid, Bertha's cigarette dangling out of her mouth – brief glimpses and impressions, like the warm-up to the main act, because suddenly there's a strong flashback to my first day of high school. I am walking the halls that smell of polish, feeling comfortable and thinking to myself, "What a nice school."

"Mr. Rato, are you OK?" I hear the doctor ask.

I say, "What?" My mind comes back to my body in the chair in the doctor's office. Again, I say, "What did you say, Doctor?"

The doctor looks at me, puts his pad down on his desk, and asks me, "Where did you just go?"

"I was having flashbacks."

"Would you like to tell me what you are thinking?"

I look away from him, get up, and walk around the room. Three words come out of my mouth.

"I don't know."

We both know that means I do know, but it's a good escape.

"Mr. Rato, please sit down. We can take things as slowly as you want. I can already see you have a lot inside, and you are having a hard time talking about certain things. Things you'd rather forget, or even wish never happened in your life. These are very real feelings, so I will never discount or deny them, and as I said, we will take this very slowly. There are no time limits."

I look out of the window.

"My family thinks I'm an abuser," I say again.

"Perfect." Not a word I would have used to describe the situation. "Can you give me a situation as an example of why they feel this way?"

I look at him and say, "You know what, I really don't know." I start to laugh. I am laughing because for the first time in my life, I have no answers. Where to start? I am holding the back of my chair, leaning forward, walking around my chair to sit down.

"Well, that's it, I guess I'm cured, right?"

We stare at each other for what seems to be forever. I look down at the floor and say, "I am totally fucked up, Doctor. My life, my past life always seems to haunt me, whatever I do, wherever I go. Why? What did I do to be treated the way I was treated?" I stop talking and look up at him.

"All these years, I always asked myself why. What did I do? What crime did I commit that I was treated like shit? Once, I was walking to my fourth period class, right? It was English. I still remember the room, the time the class started. Just the fourth period class on my first day of high school. The first three classes were great. Kids just sat around, we all listened to instructions. I go to my fourth period English class, and I go to sit down. This big kid behind me just smacks my head with his hand. I turn around, like in shock, I have no idea. 'What the fuck?' One thing, you wanted honesty, right? Well, I remember being afraid, a coward. I didn't do anything. This fucking kid, for no reason, just smacks my head and I just turn back around. I remember being afraid of not having control. You want me to be honest, right? That day was the end of my life, doctor. A new life was born on that day. That was the day I was inducted into The Bullying Club. It was a free, all-inclusive membership club of getting my ass kicked almost every day for the next four years. You wanted honesty, right? A situation told by me to you. So now, fix me so that I am not a fucked-up person anymore."

I look away, not even realizing my face is breaking up. I am trying so hard not to shed one tear. I hold my fist to my mouth, looking away again, not knowing what else to say. I feel his eyes on me as I look out of his window.

I take a deep breath, let out a long sigh, and one fucking tear escapes my eye. I quickly turn away so he can't see it rolling down my face. I wipe it off my cheek, fit myself back in the chair, sit back, and look him straight in his eyes. The door is finally open after it has been closed for forty-four years.

We look at each other. I say, "Well, are we off to a good start?"

CHAPTER 22

"Mr. Rato, a very big breakthrough has happened today."

I am realizing this man doesn't do fake, doesn't do acting. If he shows he's pleased, it's because he is, and he thinks you deserve it.

"One of the most important parts of therapy is a willingness to get help. Once that is achieved, the process can begin."

I remember the sound of the time machine making ocean waves. I recognize that we are coming to the end of our session. I can tell Doctor Silverman is pleased with what is happening.

He says, "I said I would make my recommendation for the way ahead based on today's session? Well, I think we should meet twice a week for now, on Friday and Saturday, for about a month. I think consecutive appointments will benefit you tremendously. Let's set up the exact times for next week, Friday and Saturday. Meanwhile, I want you to think about what happened today in your session. If possible, I would like you *not* to speak to anyone about it. We will revisit your past privately. I know you will be tempted to discuss things with your wife, but for now, please hold off, and you may tell her I asked you to do this. Please trust me. So, I will see you Friday of next week, and Saturday."

I watch him type on his computer, filling in the time slots for our appointments. I get up, crack a nervous smile, and adjust my clothes. I say goodbye and head for the correct door this time.

On the drive home, I think about what just happened. I am in shock. It's not that forty-four years have passed. It's that forty-four years have gone by but it feels like just yesterday. If I close my eyes, I can picture the first day of high school.

*

My first period was Science class, and it was in what they called portables. They looked like tiny little rooms framed like a house. Just imagine a bedroom-sized room with a door, chalk board and a teacher's desk and about thirty student desks. My next class was Algebra, followed by PE. Then I had lunch period and fourth period was English. After English I had Italian 101. I remember everything so vividly in my head, even after forty-four years.

I never understood why I was put into that English class. It was full of troublemakers. I guess the bad luck of the draw, or the computer just assigned the classes to each student. I remember just walking to a seat to sit down with that big fuckin' kid behind me. Now, the kid was very tall and more bulky than me, but what did I do to warrant a smack in my head? Nothing had ever happened like this before in my life. I thought it would be a one-time situation.

I learned quickly it was just the beginning. I tried the next day to sit in a different seat, but the fuckin' kid just followed right behind me. That one smack became smacks left and right with punches to my back. And then everyone was joining in. The class soon came to enjoy using my body as a punching bag.

The teacher saw what was happening and next time I walked into her class, she told me to sit in the last seat in the last row of desks. No one behind me. She hoped this would stop the bullying. Her name was Mrs. Solow. She was a young teacher and very pretty. What was funny was the fact she was very short, so the kids would say, "Hello, Mrs. Solow, you're so-o-o-o-o low." I thought it was a nice joke and she took it the right way.

She became a private friend. She saw what was happening to me. She also noticed that this class had mostly delinquent kids. One day, she took me aside.

"Hey Nick, look, I am going to be mean and tough with this group but please, just between us, don't take it as a reflection on you. I wish they were all like you. So, if I am yelling and giving out punishments it is not anything you did. And don't do the punishment assignments, OK?" She smiled and patted my shoulder. I guess she felt bad about what was happening to me.

As luck would have it, after about a month we started having substitute teachers. A full week went by, than a second week. She never returned to school. We were told that she needed a leave of absence. My savior was gone. Things quickly went back to me being the stooge of the class. This title went around the school.

*

I snap out of my memories when a car horn blares behind me,

bringing me back to the traffic lights in Manhasset. I shake my head and drive forward. The memories are vivid and strong, even after all these years. I arrive home, and Barney greets me as usual. Amelia is washing the breakfast dishes and the kids are out doing their Saturday activities.

Naturally, Amelia asks, "How did it go today?" Suddenly I'm coy. I could accept the doctor's instructions very easily. Actually putting them into practice is harder. I don't like to keep secrets from my wife.

"Uh, he, uh, told me not to discuss the session?" I manage to make it sound like a question, like I'm asking her to confirm I got it right, even when she wasn't there.

But she just takes it at face value.

"Well, if that's doctor's orders, we should respect his instructions."

I take my medication and get into bed for an afternoon nap. Barney jumps up next to me, carrying one of his dolls in his mouth. Amelia comes in to check if I need anything, and I assure her I'm fine. I turn on my side and close my eyes, hoping the medication will lull me to sleep, because I'm drifting back again forty-four years to my first day of high school.

*

That evening, the kids go out while Amelia, Barney and I stay home watching TV. Amelia is still naturally curious about my session, and sticking to the doctor's advice is hard. So I say what I can, sharing only superficial details about his office and appearance. I tell her he is handsome and has a beautiful office.

She snuggles close to me on the couch, head on my shoulder.

"Are you happy you started?"

I've been plagued with forty-four year old memories ever since that morning, but without hesitating I say, "Yes," because it's true. "I'm just sorry I didn't start sooner. But, better late than never."

We take Barney for a walk. It's one of those times when things click, and you realize you're in love and the kids are away and hey, why not? We've been married long enough to know when we're both in the mood without asking.

So, we drift home, and we drift around the house putting things away, and we drift into the bedroom.

But every time I close my eyes, my mind drifts back to that classroom. I can't get into the mood.

Eventually I kiss the top of her head and say, "I'm sorry. Can I have a rain check?" I crack a nervous smile and roll to my side of the bed.

Amelia quietly turns on her light and starts reading. Barney, sensing the moment has passed, jumps on the bed and settles at her feet. I whisper, "Good night," without turning to face her. I feel her eyes on me as I drift off.

Just as sleep takes me, I feel Amelia's hand gently touch my back. I turn to face her, and our eyes meet. She reaches over to turn off her light, and we fall asleep in each other's arms.

I wish the night was as peaceful as I've just made it sound.

CHAPTER 23

I wake up Sunday morning with a wasps' nest buzzing around in my head.

I get up out of bed slowly, turning so that my feet hit the floor. Hunched over, running my fingers through my hair many times, over and over. Amelia rests comfortably to the right of me, with Barney snoring hard in his sleep. Amelia always thinks Barney snoring to be very cute while it bothers the hell out of me.

More and more memories, images, sensations of days long gone are coming back now, extremely vivid, like they crept out overnight while I slept, backing up in my head until I could wake up and they could all come flooding forward into my consciousness. The emotional pain surrounding those days comes swirling in with them too. What was I thinking, stirring up all these memories of my high school years? Why should I throw stones at that particular nest of hornets, whipping up a swarm of feelings that will just hurt me? I thought forty-four years was a long time ago.

There seems to be no reason to put myself through this emotional war. I couldn't change the past. Why revisit those memories? Memories that scorned and belittled me my entire life?

Barney's head has risen too. His eyes follow my every move while I put on warm clothes to walk him. The warm days of summer are long gone now. Now we begin the process of adjusting ourselves for the upcoming season. It is a brisk cold Sunday morning as I walk Barney. He is thrilled to be out and about in our Manhasset neighborhood.

But I shuffle along like a zombie, my heart and feelings cold, so the coolness of the air fits perfectly with how I feel. This is exactly why I didn't want to do therapy. I had locked up all those feelings in a vault marked "Top Secret" and I threw away the key. My new-found confidence has evaporated like the illusion it was, and I am so sure I don't want to continue with Doctor Silverman.

I have made up my mind to call him. Hopefully he won't answer, and I can leave him a message. Yes, that is what I am going to do; leave a message.

Barney and I continue our walk as I fumble through my pocket to get my cell. I retrieve Doctor Silverman's phone number and position my thumb over "send". Perfect, I think. What a great way to get out of this crazy idea of going to therapy. As I start to lower my thumb to press the button, I think, I am taking the coward's way out.

My thumb bounces off the word *coward* and lifts away from the screen without making contact. I groan. Now, why did I have to use that particular word? I'm my own worst enemy.

I lift my head up and close my eyes while the word flashes behind my lids. And here come the flashbacks, images of those cowardly days flowing through the backs of my eyes – a montage that starts slowly and picks itself up to breakneck speed. Kids tripping me in the school corridors as we change classes. Taunting me, baiting, punching. *Coward.* Because I couldn't or wouldn't defend myself. I let them do it. *Coward.* The word repeats itself over and over in my head.

Suddenly, I hear my name called.

"Honey, are you OK?"

Amelia, right behind me, hauling me back from the nightmare of my past.

"I don't think I can do this, Amelia."

She takes my arm to walk along with me and Barney. There is an eerie silence between us as we walk the streets of Manhasset this Sunday morning. My head is locked in position, staring forward, Amelia looks at the ground and Barney trots happily along, breathing in the cold, brisk air.

*

The day continues as previously rehearsed a thousand times. Our family follows our normal Sunday pattern of assignments and chores. The only difference is the word *coward still lingering in my head along* with the nightmare of my high school years. It follows me all day long. I feel Amelia's eyes resting on me and sometimes my eyes lock back onto hers. I see the concern, so I try to avoid those eye-to-eye moments.

*

"I'm going to grab some bagels and a cup of coffee."

I state it as a fact to Amelia without waiting for her opinion. I grab my car keys and run out of the house.

At this point, my mind is on autopilot. Driving safely but no clear course set. I find myself almost at the entrance to Doctor Silverman's office parking lot on Northern Boulevard, the big glass cube of his building over there across the vacant space. I have no idea how I got here. All I know is that somewhere along the way I got those bagels and a cup of coffee, because they're beside me in a paper bag.

Well, I ought to find somewhere to enjoy them, so it might as well be here. I indicate and start to turn into the lot.

Nicholas is standing on the sidewalk by the entrance, just staring at me, eyes dark but face furious, like I've done something to upset him. I come to a screeching halt, and then there's a horn blaring behind me as the next car jams on its brakes. I stare at it in the rear view mirror, coming closer and closer, the driver leaning back in his seat and bracing himself for the impact that never comes. We must come within a half inch of a rear-ender, and wouldn't that look great on the insurance form? I braked because I saw this kid I see in the laundromat sometimes...

I look around and Nicholas is gone. I step out of the Lexus while the guy behind me gets going again, swerving around me and my open door, and the shout of "asshole!" is more sensed than heard over the car sound.

I gaze about in all directions, but no Nicholas. I rub my eyes, like that might make him appear from somewhere. Still no sign, and I'm halfway into the parking lot, half still stuck on the road.

I get back in and drive slowly to the nearest space.

"Oh, no! Ach!"

The bag with the coffee and the bagels, sitting on the

passenger seat, did not survive my sudden stop. It shot forward into the foot well and I can see the stain spreading over the paper as the coffee leaks through the safety cap. I pick it up quickly, holding it so it doesn't drip on me, retrieve the bagels and the cup as best I can. The bagels are mostly still dry.

I take a sip of coffee to calm down. I continue to look all around me. Nicholas is not to be found anywhere near.

I shake my head. "Nick, you're going nuts!" That's the first thought that comes into my mind. Sitting in my therapist's parking lot. If it has to happen, this is the place.

And then I'm thinking again that I just can't do this. I can't go on this therapeutic journey, and I'm a coward.

I pound the dashboard with my fist like I'm trying to hammer the idea home. I keep on thinking: why I should put myself through this? Why live through all these painful memories again? I can't take it anymore. I put my head down slowly on the steering wheel and blast out a scream.

*

I hear my cell phone ringing. My eyes open slowly, blinking hard. I'm... where? In the Lexus. In Doctor Silverman's parking lot. Where I was.

This one time, when I was a kid, I fainted in the bath. The water was hot, and I stood up too quickly, and then somehow I was lying on my back on the floor with my legs up on the tub and my feet still in the water. The water was still moving back and forth. That was how I worked out I had been out for seconds only. There was no way of knowing from my internal clock how long had passed.

Same thing now. I must have blacked out, sitting here in the car. My screams and tears broke something. How long? No idea.

I start to compose myself for consciousness. I look around, wipe my eyes and face. I hear my cell phone ring again. I see four missed calls from Amelia, and so I grab the phone quickly and answer.

"Um, hello, Amelia, is that you?" Stupid question but my mind is still a haze.

"Yes, honey, where are you?"

"Um I was just getting myself a cup of coffee and some bagels..."

Her smile comes through the phone.

"Yes, we know. We're all waiting for those bagels. It's been an hour for something that should only take you fifteen minutes. Are you OK?"

I've been out for an hour?

"Yes, um, I got to reading something on my phone. Lost track of time. I'm so sorry. I'll be home in two minutes, promise."

She says, "OK, I was just worried. Glad you're OK. See you soon."

I get myself back in the groove. Position myself to drive home – hands on wheel, feet on pedals, looking straight ahead. I get home without incident, park in the driveway and make my way into the house. My family are waiting for me. They grab the bagels and begin breakfast for themselves. I apologize again and excuse myself to go to my bedroom while Dan, Miranda and Barney do their thing in the kitchen. It means turning my back on Amelia but I just know she is staring at me. As I grab the door handle for my room, I took a quick look back and that's exactly what I see. I give her a nervous smile. She turns slowly and goes to help the kids with breakfast while I quietly close the bedroom door behind me.

We both have the same thoughts in our minds, coming at it from different directions. Can I keep going? Should I?

CHAPTER 24

McDonald's was just ahead, the golden arches standing above the roofline of the shops, people going in through the glass doors empty handed and coming out with brown paper bags. Time to put the act on. Nicholas put the cigarette to his lips and breathed in cautiously. He had got the hang of it now, though the first attempts had made him cough and hack and wheeze and made him feel ill. It still tasted foul but now it didn't feel like someone was scrubbing the inside of his throat with sandpaper.

Anyway, it didn't matter what smoking felt like. What mattered was how it looked. Nicholas had worked that out, watching the older kids, the ones who were popular, the ones who led the pack, the ones whom no one would ever dare bully. If he could look like them, act like them, then maybe the bullying would stop. He wouldn't impress the bullies – he had given up on that – but he might make some powerful friends. He would be very happy just to shelter in their social shadow. Let the predators prowl around outside but not dare approach.

But there was no point being a cool smoker if no one saw you doing it, and if he did it at school then he would just get busted by a teacher.

So, McDonald's it was. Zero teachers to interfere, and

plenty of his peers around to see him.

Obviously, he wouldn't go in there smoking. He would just get thrown out again. No, he had practiced the move in advance. Casually throw the stub to the ground, grind it out with his foot, keep walking through the doors, all in one smooth movement, just like in the movies. He glanced ahead at the paving in front of the store. There was a slab there with a chip missing from one corner. That was his target. He would chuck the cigarette down just there.

His eyes wandered to the waist-high bin outside the store. He had been brought up not to litter and suddenly he was feeling guilty about Plan A. Was it too late for a Plan B? Stub the cigarette out on the top of the bin and chuck it in along with the crumpled bags and polystyrene boxes?

And suddenly it was all academic, moot, irrelevant, because coming the other way and heading for the same destination was a group of kids from school.

"Hey, guys, look at the fucking fem smoking!"

And just like that the plan lay in tatters. What the hell had he been thinking?

The other kids were laughing. The one who had shouted was now flapping his wrist like it was limp and fake puffing out smoke.

"Look at the fag, look at the fag!"

There was one last choice, apart from running to get the hell out of here. Get inside, get in front of witnesses. Nicholas knew from experience not to trust the kindness of strangers, and if these kids carried on acting out in there then he couldn't rely on anyone to intervene. But just the presence of other people might stop them trying it in the first place.

There was no more thought of grinding the cigarette out and looking cool. He chucked it down on the ground and sped up, walking towards the doors twice as fast. It was just a numbers game now. If he got there faster than they did...

He didn't. They also accelerated and surrounded him just a few tantalizing feet from the glass.

One of them tripped him up and he stumbled into the wall of the building, slapping his hands painfully against the bricks as the price of not going head over ass onto the concrete. He scrambled to his feet before they could close around him.

There was one more option and it briefly flashed through his mind. Fight back. If he dived forward then he could probably get one of them with his head. Or he could swing a fist and hurt one of them before they all piled onto him in return.

But as he had learned the time he hit the kid with the book, there was no point. It just made them even more vindictive the next time they caught up with him.

So he did the only thing left to him, and fled.

"Hey, fuckin' fairy, don't run, fly away!" the mocking calls followed him. "You're a fuckin' asshole!"

The sound of their laughter faded into the slapping of his feet on the ground as he fled the scene in humiliation, eyes streaming, all his carefully gathered dignity in shreds.

CHAPTER 25

All week I have buyers' remorse about seeing this therapist. I think of every excuse in the book to try to convince myself to cancel. As the next scheduled day looms closer and closer my desire to not keep my appointment grows stronger, and my ability to think up plausible excuses as to why not steadily declines.

When the day finally arrives to see Doctor Silverman, I spend the whole morning getting ready for the session, and as I'm well out of plausible excuses by now, I try to convince myself with increasingly crazy excuses not to show up.

And yet, I find myself pulling into a parking space at the doctor's office. The same man greets me as I enter the building. All I say is "Good morning" and I continue straight back and to the right. It is always the same man, I think as I turn the handle to enter Doctor Silverman's office – that's three visits in a row.

I know the drill. I get myself a bottle of water and make myself as comfortable as I can, when I am still so nervous. I know that if I really commit to this then I couldn't go back.

My whole life I have been taught that going to see this kind of doctor makes you appear weak, unmanly. I know this will sound funny, but my family would believe that anyone who wanted to see a psychiatrist should have his head examined.

You see, I told you that would sound funny. As I take some water, I hear Doctor Silverman's office door open. I turn and say hello to the doctor. He guides me in and I make myself comfortable in the same chair as I sat last week.

"Doctor Silverman, I still feel apprehensive about these sessions."

The doctor looks at me in that way I am getting used to. One day I might say something so shocking that it will elicit some kind of reaction, but that day must be a long way away.

"Ninety nine point nine percent of people have the same feelings," he says. "But there are two important things that I need to know from a patient at the beginning. First, even if you're scared or nervous, do you believe that this method, this route you have chosen to adjust your life, is a good idea? Even if you're scared?"

I can only tell him the truth. I've seen the alternative.

"I am apprehensive, but I do want to start this program."

He asks the second question.

"I told you when we first met that I cannot change you, the person. In fact, I can guarantee it. That is a misconception of what I do. It's a popular one but that doesn't make it any less wrong. So, you need to admit to me that you're not looking to change who you are, or for any type of quick fix. My office, my job, and my goals for my patients are to get them to understand their situations, and to help them achieve a peaceful, happy life of their own. It is important that you tell me now before we begin that these are the results you are expecting to achieve."

He has addressed one of the fears behind my reluctance about coming. It's not just the opening up of the hornet's nest in my head – though that is a large part of it. It's that I will lose *me*. Love it or hate it, that hornet's nest defines me. What would I be without it? I have grown too attached to my identity to want to lose it.

But, turns out I don't lose it at all. I just get to see it differently. OK, I can work with that.

"I guess I did believe I would come to these sessions to change. I'm glad you explained how the process works."

We both make ourselves comfortable and stare at one another.

"So, what is my next step? Am I supposed to start to cry?"

Before he can answer, I get up from my chair and walk around the room.

"You know, Doctor, this is so difficult. For some reason I thought this would be easier. I don't know what you are waiting for."

The doctor starts to write on his pad. Once again, the room grows silent. I keep pacing.

"How does this start? I wish you'd take the lead, Doctor."

The doctor replies, "Nick, I am waiting for you to take down your defenses. I see you, here in my office, but when you sit it's like you want to be elsewhere, or you walk about as if my questions can't catch you that way. It is like you're in defensive mode when I need you to be open to express your real self. Right now, all your energy is focused on putting up a wall to try and protect yourself. I can see that any question I ask, you will immediately deflect. We can start as soon as I see you make a conscious effort to be totally open. I need to see that there are no walls between us. This way you will give me the right information that I will need to give you an analysis of your life."

My circuit of the room takes me past a portrait of a beautiful old ship. I know hardly anything about ships but it catches my eye.

"This is a fine piece," I say. "See how the sails are straining in the wind? And that burst of spray around the front – uh, the bows – it's like the artist snapped it just as it burst through that wave. You can tell, this is a ship that is going somewhere in a hurry. Maybe it's on an urgent mission. Maybe it just wants to get home. But no, hold on, it's sailing away from the coast. So it's leaving port, I guess. Where is that coast, I wonder? Cape Cod? Somewhere in Massachusetts anyway, I guess." I stand back and survey it critically, my head on one side.

The doctor says, "This is a perfect example. I am waiting for you to talk about your life, and you want to talk about a portrait of a ship that is on my wall."

I wheel on him.

"*Fine!* You wanna know what the fuck my life is all about? Why don't you take that pen and shove it up your ass! You know I'm already sick and tired of these sessions. It's like you're so *reasonable* all the time. Everything here so far reminds me of some stereotypical therapist session on TV. It's like a bullshitting waste of time. My time here and you getting paid. It's all B.S. You know what, I'm getting the hell out of here."

I grab my things and head for the door.

"Nick, wrong door – you need to leave from that door in the back."

I stare at him.

"Are you kidding me? You're worried what door I was

leaving from? You don't care that I just blew up in your office, wanting to leave?"

"Nick, I told you these sessions will not help you until you are completely willing to give one hundred percent of your being into this process. And since you're not at that point, go ahead and leave."

I am stunned, shocked to the core that he is not even trying to stop me from leaving. I walk to the door and just stand there, wanting to go. Thinking, why isn't he trying to stop me, why isn't he trying to make me see the light? I stay at the doorway, half in the room and half out. My head hanging down, embarrassed how I just acted.

The worst thing happens. I had promised myself not to shed one tear. I break. I have my face turned downward and slowly I break. The strong exterior being, the defensive soul, the coldhearted feelings that I locked up for the last forty-four years finally shatter like a glass vase hitting the floor, its remnants flying out all over the floor in the office, the arch of the door frame, the outer hallway beyond his office.

I don't realize I am crying hysterically. My face is in my hands. Time seems to have stopped. For a moment I don't know what, where, how and why I am in a man's office.

I feel a gentle touch of the doctor's hand on my shoulder. It brings me back to reality. With his other hand he guides me back into the room, closes the door and asks me to sit down. I look up at the doctor.

"Why did they treat me the way they did back in high school? I didn't do anything but go to school and try to make friends in a new school year. Why did I have to go through that mental and physical abuse, Doctor?"

He looks at me gently across the desk.

"Why not give me an example?"

CHAPTER 26

I had such big ideas about how great high school was going to be. And they lasted until that fourth period class, English, on Day One. My grand dreams and plans were shattered on my first day of classes and the next four years just ground them into smaller and smaller pieces.

"Kids, boys, girls, both would just trip me from behind as I walked," I tell him. "Hitting my head hard as I was sitting in my seat or walking to a classroom. Kids came right up to me, close to my face, saying, 'You're so ugly, why don't you kill yourself?'"

I am so embarrassed how fucked up I am, crying. A grown man crying like a fuckin' baby.

"And, Doctor, the more I tried to make myself inclusive, the more they pushed me away. Sometimes I would try to fight back and that made things worse. They became more vicious, nastier, hit harder. If they couldn't hit me harder at that moment then they remembered all too well the next day and they caught up then."

I see the doctor taking a lot of notes. Forty-four years of abuse has just started pouring out, with more to come. My life that I kept closed, completely hidden safely so no one could see. The door has opened and the ghosts are released. I don't know what else to say. I wipe my face with some tissues next to my chair. I look up at Doctor Silverman.

"So, is this what you wanted to hear from me?" I look down at my feet, wipe my eyes and nose one more time and take a deep breath. I know it's just the beginning but it is so much more hurtful, more painful than I expected it to be. I have a bad feeling that things are going to get even worse in later sessions.

"*Why* did I have to go through those horrible years? What did I do except get up and go to my classes? What makes one human being enjoy making another human suffer with insults and physical violence? Those kids took away what were supposed to be the best years of my life. The worst part about it is that I didn't do anything to deserve being treated the way I was treated."

I look again at the doctor.

"Do you know what bothers me the most? How everyone around me didn't do a damn thing to help. Didn't want to get involved. The other kids just walked around me or joined in the fun of beating me up. *And*, when this one kid did decide to help me..."

Another breath.

"The favorite thing to do to me on a daily basis was to knock all my books out of my hands as we changed classes. So, I used to tie a rubber thingamajig around my books that kind of helped because than the books all fell in one big dump. Once, though, they all went flying and this kid..."

Tom Baxter. A name I haven't thought of in four decades.

"He bent down to help me pick them up, and I was more

upset with him than the actual bullies. I just grabbed my things and tried to hold on to my dignity. I didn't even thank him for his help. Can you believe it? I was like, leave me alone, I don't need your help. I know I was more embarrassed than ungrateful, but my first reaction was to push him away, the one kid who tried to intervene."

So many new memories flooding back, but they're all fuel for the consuming fire of the one big question in my mind, the one I've had all these years: *why?* Why did this happen to me? Why, Why, Why?

I am waiting for some answers, some explanations, but all I get is, "Our time is done. Let's pick up tomorrow morning, Saturday, same time as last week?"

I give the doctor a short smile and head out of his office in the direction of the correct door.

CHAPTER 27

The whole week goes by with a cloud looming over me every fuckin' day. This is exactly what I didn't want to happen to my life. I just know that bringing up these old memories will also bring back how I felt at that time. I already have the bad memories in my head. Reliving it all again makes the pain real, and it still hurts. It takes a lot to relive it, talk about it to a total stranger and then go home again, still feeling the pain, keeping it until my next appointment.

My whole life has been about trying to have closure on that time in my life. Every day for those four years crushed me. Those so called "wonder years"! That fuckin' TV show starts with happy memories, children running around during summertime weather, having barbecues – it's all bullshit. I just want to erase that time of my life, somehow, but I can't seem to find how.

*

Getting myself to the laundromat today is more difficult than usual. I'm moving through molasses. My limbs are heavier, steering wheel is less responsive, the pedals are stiffer, the car is more sluggish. Eventually I park and make my way to the machine I like to use, with my favorite chair waiting for me beside it. I get the laundry started, sit down with my legs straight out and my arms crossed in front, blow out a long sigh of air. I hear the door of the public rest room shut behind me. It's good old Bertha and that fine cigarette dangling out of her mouth. She decides to make herself comfortable next to me. I start to say hello back to her hello, and I'm getting ready to add will she please just leave me alone today, but after just the hello she cuts me off.

"So, I can tell you've been to see my friend the doctor? You know how I can tell, Mac? Because you got that face. That is the face I had too, my first visits with the good Doc."

I try to get another word in edgewise, but I only get as far as, "Look, Bertha," and she jumps in again.

"Seems like it's working. If you're feeling sick, like something looming over you this whole week – well, my friend, you had a great first visit. You see, think about it. If you came in today feeling good about yourself, smiling, having no pains, no frustration with life, you wasted a session. This is the beginning of the crap you are going through. You gotta understand that whatever you are speaking about with the Doc, it might take years to go over, so give yourself at least some months, weeks too, just to get started."

I open my mouth but it is no use. She just keeps chiming in.

"I had a shit too." I begin to frown, puzzled. "Not in my ass but in my life. You think you have the maurket on being the only one on Earth that has shit going on inside their head? Think about what I am saying, OK? Just think about it. And stop feeling sorry for yourself while you are at it. So, you got shit in your life added to the shit up your ass. You are going to get rid of it, trust me. That shit stuck up in your ass didn't get there overnight, so don't be so hard on yourself. Give this doc a shot, give him time, give him your gratitude, then pay his high prices."

She gives me a big smile with her cigarette dangling out of her mouth. She hits my shoulder and I go flying to the left.

"That's some left hook you got there, Bertha."

She answers, "Yeah, been told that my whole life."

*

The dryer is humming, and the sound puts me into a sleep-like trance until the dryer alarm goes off.

I go by Bertha's office to say goodbye. I was about to tell her thank you and once again she doesn't allow me to talk.

"No thanks, nothing, it isn't necessary. Just keep doing what you are doing with good old Doc, keep feeling what you're feeling. One day it will all make sense, and you will feel better."

I start to leave but she gives me one more piece of advice.

"Hey Mac, whatever is your beef going on, realize one thing – it isn't ever going to go away. You gotta accept that now. I tell you what, Mac – you will learn to live with it better than you are right now. That is all we people do, you, me, the others in this free membership that we got put into. It's non-refundable. Just know that you are starting to make some rules, some changes too, the more you work with good old Doc, so you can enjoy membership privileges. You got my meaning, Mac? Have a good night, see you next week."

Driving home I think about what Bertha said to me today. I am going to put my soul into Doctor Silverman's hands. I will trust him and his sessions completely.

CHAPTER 28

"All of a sudden, this kid had me in a choke hold in one of the stalls. My first week of classes, in the men's room. I was totally in shock. Nothing ever happened like this before. We both struggled in that limited space. I remember my left hand just trying to do anything, splashing some toilet water. The kid let me go, guess I was struggling too much for him. You know, I think he was in a state himself because he just stopped. We both just stood there for what seemed to be a long time, when it was seconds."

I stop to look out of Doctor Silverman's office window. It's a grayish, cold day, my third week into these sessions. "I tried to open the door latch, and the kid hit my hand, knocking it away from opening and stopping me running out of the men's room."

I look straight into Doctor Silverman's eyes and tell him what the kid said next.

"He said, 'Fuckin' faggot, give me that chain.'"

It happened so fast, feeling my gold chain going over my head. I still remember the struggle to get it off my neck. I fell backwards into the toilet, ending up sitting on the rim. Then he was struggling to escape himself. He was so nervous to get out, he struggled to get the latch off. After a few seconds he got the door open and made his escape. I just sat there, still messed up about the whole situation.

"Why didn't I fight back or do anything? I was a fuckin' coward! I did nothing, I did nothing, I did *nothing!*"

I stop talking. I get up and walk around the room. I run my fingers through my hair and rest both hands on my face. I look back to see the doctor writing notes. I say the next three words extremely slowly in front of him.

"*I – did – no – thing!*"

I put my hands in my pocket.

"Doctor, after this incident the only thing that bothered me was feeling cowardly. It made me feel worse than the mugging. I didn't think of the injustice that just happened to me; I didn't think of the value of the gold chain. In fact, my mother gave my dad that chain on their honeymoon in Italy. All these things, never once in my mind. The only thought I had was, what a fuckin' coward. The faggot coward I was that morning on my first week of high school."

I drop back into the chair. The memory is forty-four years old and I feel like it just happened twenty minutes ago.

"After a full year, Doctor, I finally told my parents what had happened that morning. I had to give them a reason why I wanted to go to a Catholic private school instead of that public high school. That whole year was horrible. So, I had to start telling them some of the things that went on there. They both acted like I predicted. My dad made fun of me. In fact, the only thing worse than how I felt, even more than feeling like a coward, was the disapproving look in my dad's eyes. Like he also thought I was a faggot coward. That was worse than feeling like a coward myself. Then I had to look into my mother's eyes and I saw all the love she had for me, all the *pity*, that 'Oh, my poor baby' as she tried to comfort me. That's all my dad needed to see, and then *he* started on *her*, saying the emotions she was displaying were the reason I am the way I am, a faggot coward."

I look directly into the doctor's eyes, waiting for some words of wisdom. Words that I am paying for, to help deal with the feelings I have inside. I wait and nothing comes out of his mouth. I think what a waste of time this is all turning out to be. He takes some more notes and waits a few minutes.

"After you talked with your parents, what happened next?"

"My brothers came into the picture, and they took it the way my dad did. They all thought, except my mother, that I was a fuckin' loser, faggot coward and my mother's pity just made me feel even worse. I wished I had never told them anything. When I think back to those days, I still feel the same shame, the same embarrassment. If I could have died at that moment, if I'd had the option, I would have chosen it. Now I get it, how some teenagers turn to suicide. I mean, I was a fuckin' coward too when it came to trying to commit suicide. I couldn't even do that right."

Doctor Silverman writes some more notes.

"Do you still feel suicidal thoughts? I need to know truthfully, now."

I give one of those nervous smiles.

"No, Doctor, I didn't do it then and I'm not thinking of doing something like that now. All I am saying is that I can understand why people would do such a horrible thing as suicide."

He writes down some more notes.

"I am glad to hear that."

I turn to the window again to get away from his stares and notice it is raining.

"Well, I guess poor Barney is going to miss his walk today."

Doctor Silverman keeps writing notes.

"And how did it end up, this time when you talked to your parents about changing schools?"

I tell him exactly what happened.

"I left the family gathering to go to my room. I heard my brothers laughing and my dad being pissed off, the big Italian tough guy that he acts like. Shutting my door on them felt good, like I was shutting out their judgments. I already had my self-loathing. I didn't need any more of those feelings. Later, my mother came into my room and told me that she would pay for me to go to private school."

I breathe out.

"I should have been happy, but that day and the way it ended, they left me worse off. I thought families were supposed to help you. I didn't get any support from any of them, except my mother's pity, which I didn't want. I wanted them to support me and give me encouragement. All anyone accomplished that day was making me feel worse about myself."

*

The wave machine is making the sounds that say our session is coming to an end.

"Well, I'll see you for our appointment tomorrow."

I gather up all my things. I am walking to the door when he

does his Columbo act, asks me just one more thing.

"If you had to relive that moment of being mugged in the bathroom, being the person you are today, would you do anything different?"

I stop with my hand on the door.

"You mean, how I would react if I could live that moment of time as the kind of person I am today?"

"Yes. Your honest answer."

I can't go there now.

"I'll think about it and give you an answer tomorrow."

As I walk to my car, the rain begins to come down harder. I don't care. I walk, not fucking caring about anything. Thinking about that day all over again made me feel horrible. The feelings of self-loathing, being a faggot coward, my dad and brothers making fun of me, and my mother's pity all work together with the rotten weather. The rain is the perfect ending to another fucked-up day in my life.

I slam the car door shut and start up the Lexus, and think again that forty-four years have passed. Forty-four years. Forty-four years, and the rain drums on the roof. And as the rain hits the ground, I hit my head against the steering wheel.

CHAPTER 29

"Why don't you ask me what you really want to ask? Am I still a coward?"

Trying to dodge a bullet I know will be coming soon, I get up from the chair and walk over to the window of the doctor's office.

Doctor Silverman had opened with a perfectly simple question. "Did you think about what I asked you to think about last night at home? How would you react today, right now, if someone tried to take you into a stall and mug you?"

As usual, I change the subject.

"Wait, didn't I do the same thing yesterday? Walk up and look outside? A way to avoid talking or thinking. Kind of like trying to kill time. You know your parking lot is huge? Did you know that, Doctor?"

But I know I'm out of excuses, so I walk back to my chair. I don't sit.

Doctor Silverman says, "I am glad you like my offices, the views, the large parking space. Well? Did you think about it?"

"Me at this age or me at fourteen with all my extra forty-four years life experience? I can't answer your question. You answer mine. You want to know if I feel like a coward?"

Doctor Silverman makes some more notes.

"I am not going to address your questions, your suspicions, what people think of you. You need to interpret your feelings and help yourself deal with them. Do you feel scared to stand up to someone? It's OK to say it."

I make an effort to engage.

"I don't know. I mean I just don't know. I am a man, and I shouldn't feel that way, right? I think if my wife, my kids, my dog even, would ever be in trouble, I know I would jump through fire for any one of their lives." That bit I know to be one hundred percent true, and it gives me confidence to press on to a less than satisfying conclusion. "But me for myself, in truth I don't feel that strong love for myself and that's the truth."

I sit back down. That's how I feel about myself.

A couple of minutes pass.

"Anything else you want to ask me?"

Doctor Silverman makes more notes, positions himself in his chair.

"I want to know why you can stand up for the people you love but when it comes to you, you feel you cannot stand up for yourself."

I run my hands through my hair. I need to massage my scalp, to get those thought processes flowing. He's asking questions that are making sense. It's only right to respond.

"I don't know, Doctor. I feel out of control when I have to stand up for myself. I become unable to control certain body functions, like, I start to tremble, I start to not be able to breathe right. It's like my body is doing things to itself without me having control. This time at a formal birthday party, my cousin started yelling at me and I knew if I wanted to, I could smash a chair on top of her. I mean I'm normally not afraid, but my body just shut down on its own, not knowing what to do. I had to ask my wife to walk me out of the formal event area and as we were walking, I was trembling. My whole body was taken over by a force in which I had no control."

And the cowardice thing? I think.

"And I can honestly say I had zero fear – cowardly fear – I would have loved to yell back or throw something for making herself look like an ass. But I didn't do anything, as I said."

I feel the doctor asked me a good question but truthfully, I just don't know how I would react now.

"I *think* probably everything would go down the same way." More silence. "That whole year at public high school, things would happen to me over and over. I guess kids talk and I walked around with a target on my back. That's why I wanted to change schools. I thought by going to a private school I wouldn't have the same experiences. And for six months, that was true."

I look at him sideways.

"When I told my father that I was happy at the private school, you know what he said? 'The broom always sweeps good in the beginning.' I was in shock that he had to ruin that little bit of happiness I thought I was going to have. But, in the end, he was right because after six months things started to happen to me like they did at the public school. I knew by then I was destined to go through all my high school years like this.

"I just don't know why, Doctor. All these years I kept thinking, *why?* I was an introvert, I never said or did anything, I just would attend my classes and go home. But, Doctor, truthfully it was the worst four years of my life and not only in school. I had to come home to my family, my father, my brothers, and live with their own mean comments.

"Funny, as soon as I graduated from high school and attended college the whole harassment just stopped. From day one until all the way up to graduation, there was no one pushing me around. It just completely stopped.

"But what's fuckin' funny, Doctor, is that when I got engaged to Amelia, her friends were friends with the mean kids that fucked me up for years! What the hell luck that I had to keep seeing some of them at my wife's friends' house! And oh, they made sure everyone had the right story. They talked to my wife, they corrected what had happened to me, telling all the lies and stories the way they wanted Amelia to believe. They admitted to me that they didn't like me. They said that to me right to my face, when they had a private moment with me. And they continued to exploit the situation and repeat all the things that happened to me. Amelia didn't know. I don't think I ever told her they were doing this before we got married. Fucked up, right, Doc?"

Doctor Silverman is actually looking surprised. Maybe at how small the world is, and how all my childhood crap quite literally followed me into adulthood.

"I... can see you really got a raw deal, and I must admit it was unfortunate that, yes, it came back again with your new friend, to be your new wife. I understand how this would just compound your problems and how the effect lingered into your family and raising your children."

"Oh, I'll tell you the truth, Doctor. My wife didn't

understand but she was always supportive of my feelings, and she never made me feel less of a man, and I never felt she looked down on me. She was warm and loving no matter how mean her friends were."

We both just sit there once more, until that machine makes that noise again, ending our session.

"I just don't understand *why* I had all those years of pain and suffering. Worse, why I left school to go home and I had to feel uncomfortable there too – after school in my own home, Doctor!"

A breath.

"Same time same days next week?"

I gather my stuff and go to the correct door. I start to open it and then I turn around to ask Doctor Silverman the same one-word question again that I have been asking myself for forty-four years.

"WHY?"

CHAPTER 30

Why?

A blaring car horn snaps me out of it, briefly. The traffic light has turned green, and I haven't noticed because that fuckin' word has stayed in my head the whole time I walked from the doctor's office to my car and then the whole way driving home.

The driver behind me has noticed, and must have been watching the light very intensely because he holds the horn down for what seems to be a lifetime.

"All right! All right, asshole, I'll go!"

I put the car into drive and pull away. My hand is sore. I have been banging my fist on the steering wheel in time with the chant: *why why why why why?*

I still don't know myself, I just say *why?* Just like I have been doing these last forty-four years.

I am driving home but it is like the car is on autopilot. It is driving itself with me behind the steering wheel. I have no real location in mind.

Why? for some reason just stays in my head the whole drive home. Why is *why?* doing that to me? It just will not go away.

I get home and go into the kitchen and there is my best buddy that we all know and love, Barney. I get his things together to take him for his walk.

"Barney, *why*, yes, *why* do you love me?"

He runs up and down the kitchen floor with his toy in his mouth. He has wonderful dolls and each week he has a favorite doll he likes the best. Next week it will be another. I ask him again and all he can do is just be happy, because he is with someone who he lives with and that is how he is.

I'm still thinking *why*? as we walk out of the house. *Why* couldn't life be as simple as Barney feels and lives it?

*

Doctor Silverman starts.

"How was your week, Nick?"

The week has gone by so fast. We both have a routine that is familiar after a month of sessions and we go into it.

I answer, "Uneventful, Doctor, nothing to discuss. Life goes on around me as if I just exist. I don't know what else to tell you."

I pause. I've issued the standard disclaimer, now it's time to say something useful.

"That word, *why*, stayed on my mind all week. It's crossed my mind many times before but this week it stuck in my thoughts much more than usual. I don't think it's fair for *anyone* to have a life like that in high school. It's still happening today. Not to me, no, but nothing has changed – the kids with the same destiny as mine go on living each day and they get it too. Now, instead of 'Why me?' I think why does this happen to certain children. It's just not right, Doctor."

I see the doctor taking notes.

Doctor Silverman says, "You may never get a real answer about that word, and if that happens to be the case, can you live with that?"

I think about it for a second.

"Well, I guess if I've lived to fifty-eight thinking about the word and being able to exist, I guess so."

I walk around the room again, looking at things in the office. I just don't know what else to do.

The doctor smiles.

"I'm happy you came to that conclusion. People think that going to therapy is a fix-all magical session for our minds. That is not the case. These sessions are to help people accept certain realities that have occurred or will occur or are just present in the now. To understand and accept that we may never get answers to our 'why' questions, to live and know it. How do you feel now that you know that there isn't an answer to all of life's coming and goings?"

I say what I realize to be true.

"I feel a certain relief, a certain weight off my back. It makes sense that we can't answer every question or even expect an answer. Also, I guess I'm not entitled to get answers? I felt for years that I had the right to have certain liberties and that was wrong."

And then it bursts out.

"But it hurts so much, Doctor! The pain of those days is still so real to me."

I sit down in the chair and look directly into his eyes as I talk.

"I can close my eyes, Doctor, and I can still see those

horrible days vividly in my head. I get lost back in them. They were supposed to be the best years of my life. You know..." I start to wipe a tear from my face and I give him a nervous smile. "I guess you're right that knowing there aren't any real answers to the 'why?' word is a comfort to my soul." I force a laugh and say, "I guess I should stop feeling sorry for myself. That must be the best way to look at the 'why' question." I wipe more tears away and make myself more comfortable in the chair. There is silence now between us. I cough and say, "Excuse me." Doctor Silverman writes some more notes and puts his pen down.

"Nick, I want you to share this month's experiences with your wife and children. Take notes, or even video the conversation you have. Tomorrow we can discuss the family meeting."

*

So, I got some answers today on questions that I have been struggling with for years. I don't feel better about our session today but it gave me a better understanding of what I should expect from my life experiences. Unfortunately, nature doesn't owe anything to anyone. I now understand that there are no guarantees or expectations that I should expect from life. I took it for granted that you're born and such and such things should happen. You get to a certain age and once again expect such and such should happen. I was living very stupidly, expecting to receive.

When I get home there is Barney, just waiting for me or I guess anyone to come home. He knew someone would and he was grateful to know that one of us would come and help make his life happy. His innocence of our world, his happiness, his love is such a great comfort to my family. Him running back and forth with his doll of the week in his mouth, his happiness and readiness to go out for a walk – they are wonderful moments which I wish I could savor all day long. How I wish that I could bottle these feelings up and take it as a pill form. I would pay any amount to have that created for me.

"Let's go, Barns, let's go!"

Realizing that will never happen is the first step I needed to achieve some kind of peace in my life.

But, I think as I watch Barney walking, I know the road that I still need to walk ahead is a long one.

CHAPTER 31

Barney was butting his head against her knee. He was wondering why everyone was sitting around the kitchen table but no one was doing the most important thing they did when they did that, which was provide him with food.

Amelia absently put a hand down to scratch between his ears and watched Nick fiddle with the phone, trying to set it up so that the camera would capture the three of them. Next to her was Miranda, and next to Miranda was Daniel, all three of them bunched together rather than spacing themselves around the table at ninety degree angles like they usually did. The kids were looking at their father from under their brows, so like they did when they were having a teenage grump about being made to do something that Amelia longed to hug them because she could easily have forgotten they were both in their twenties.

And she was curious herself, to see what this was all about.

It had been alarming, to say the least, when Nick strode in, fresh from his session, and announced, "Right, we're having a family conference." But she guessed he wouldn't do it without a good reason. In fact, she sensed the presence of a fragile resolve behind this that could evaporate at any moment. If Nick thought that a family conference was a good idea, then it probably was, and they should do it before he changed his mind.

Daniel had been absorbed in some kind of game in his room and had just looked at her reproachfully when she indicated with signals that his presence was needed. But he had set aside his earphones and followed after her, hands in his pockets.

Miranda...

"What?" Glaring up at her from her books and her laptop. "He just comes in and says, right, everyone in the kitchen right now, and we're just expected to do it, like, we couldn't possibly have any plans of our own?"

Amelia had just looked at her, and so she had made a great show of huffing and puffing and folding the laptop shut, and then following her mother to the kitchen, even more reluctantly than her brother.

Nick slid into the chair on her other side, not taking his eyes off the screen.

"Scoot round a bit, Dan..."

"You could just turn the camera?" Miranda suggested.

"But then your Mom would be out of shot..."

Eventually the camera was set up to his satisfaction. Nick cleared his throat.

"Right..." He looked around at each of them, and for the first time he might have sensed they were put out by his manner. "Uh, thank you. Thank you for doing this at such short notice."

His hands were clasped together and he was slowly tapping the table in front of him. Amelia saw that Daniel had noticed this. His head didn't move from its chin-down position but his eyes were following the movement, up, down, up, down.

Miranda just said, "So, family selfie-time couldn't wait until after dinner?"

"It's something Doctor Silverman said." Nick started talking before Miranda had finished saying "dinner". Amelia wondered if he had even heard her. "And he wants me to record it. So."

He reached over and tapped the red circle "record" icon on the screen.

"So, we don't get a say about being recorded?" Miranda asked. "Aren't you meant to ask for consent nowadays?" Again Nick showed no sign of even hearing. It was unlike him just to ignore people, even when he was at his worst. Amelia wondered if he was running through a prepared script in his head, anxious to get to the end of it before his courage failed. So, he was also worried that he might not make it through whatever this was. Miranda was looking around, trying to get a hint of support from the rest of her family. Amelia caught her eye and gave a very slight shake of the head. Miranda subsided, a little, sitting back.

"He wants me to... tell you," Nick said. "About. What happened to me. When I was a kid."

They waited. They waited some more. Amelia cocked an eye at the counter on the screen which showed how long the phone had been recording. 1:25... 26... 27...

"The thing is, things... happ–... happened to..."

She could hear his throat closing up, denying the words passage. He coughed, got up, took a drink of water, brought the glass back to the table and sat down without checking his position on the camera. Amelia guessed it didn't matter if he wasn't in the picture. It was still recording his words.

"Okay. Start at the beginning. High school. Year one. Day one. The f–... the fir–..." Another swallow of water. "The first few periods were fine. First, second, third. Then the f–... four–... fourth, I sit down and... this... this guy..."

His voice disappeared into a breathless croak. No one moved or said a word. Amelia looked at the counter. 2:13... 14... 15...

Empathetic Daniel made a guess as to what was happening.

"Dad, is it... is it too painful? Is that why you can't talk? I mean, we appreciate you trying this, to level with us, but Uncle Tony did tell us a lot already about the crap you went through, so we can, you know, fill in the blanks ourselves, if you like."

"No." For the first time Nick sounded in command. "No, you have to hear it from me."

Miranda rolled her eyes.

"So even now you're getting therapy, it's all about you, right? Forget it, Dad. Write it down and I'll read it later."

She started to push her chair back as a prelude to getting up. She never made it. Before she was half way back, Nick had started talking. Looking down, staring at the table top, speaking in a dull monotone, a voice Amelia had never heard before, and it pinned everyone to their seats. An A.I. at the end of the phone had more personality. Every hint, every nuance, every iota of what made Nick, Nick was gone. This voice was pure fact.

It was their own imaginations that provided the emotion, the horror, as he carefully, meticulously, forensically described four years of hell on Earth. Tony had sketched it out for them but now, for the first time ever, they got the full picture. Colored in, touched up, layered with fine shades and textures, finished and varnished.

There was no winding up, no slowing down, no coming to a conclusion. The only sign that Nick had come to the end was when he stopped talking because he had run out of facts to relate. The faucet had run dry, the tank was empty. He still stared down at the table and his clasped hands continued to beat the top, a slow, metronomic rhythm, a beat only he could hear. Maybe it was his heart, Amelia thought, just because she wanted to think something that wasn't to do with what she had just heard.

She didn't look at the recording counter but it was well into double figures.

"... Wow," Daniel breathed. Even more quietly, barely a whisper, Miranda breathed out.

"... Shit..."

Nick didn't move. Just stared at the table, clasped hands tapping. Amelia reached out slowly, gently, covered them with her own hand, pressing down to stifle the beat. The rest of him didn't move. She studied his profile as though it hid secrets she had never noticed before.

"Thank you, Nick. Thank you."

Daniel grunted something that could have been seconding her.

Nick slowly looked up, turned his head to each of them one at a time.

"Are there any questions?"

Miranda sat back, hands pushed into her pockets, shaken but rallying.

"So..." She took a breath. "Are you going to keep seeing this guy?"

CHAPTER 32

Two days turn into a week turn into another week turn into a month. Time clicks on, month passing into another month eight times over, all through the fall and Christmas and the New Year and the slow up-shift into spring. Time goes on no matter if you're ready or not. All of us are subject to its pushy way of living on this Earth. It has zero tolerance for anyone else.

I'm still going to Doctor Silverman, and I'm still going to the laundromat. This is an unofficial part of my healing. Self-diagnosed and self-prescribed. I haven't mentioned it to Silverman. I mean, he knows about it because he knows I know Bertha, but he doesn't know – I haven't told him – just how much it means to me. If he thinks of it at all, it might be that my washing machine broke and so I went to the laundromat and met one of his patients there, but then my washing machine got fixed and so I stopped. But I haven't stopped. I don't know how but I know I would miss it if I did.

So, we still don't have a washing machine. It's become a family joke. The family are used to my laundry days – they'd miss them too if they stopped – and it gets me out of the house and out of their hair for a guaranteed couple of hours a week, so they let it go.

Sometimes I see the kid, Nicholas, off in the distance, around the park or around town, but the boy seems to be lying low. I remember seeing him lurking at the entrance to Doctor Silverman's car parking lot that time and I remember the way he glared at me. That was one seriously pissed kid. Does he maybe feel resentful of me, because I'm getting help that he can't? But there's not much I can do if I don't even know where Nicholas lives, or how to find him.

And I have something more important to worry about. The summer is just around the corner once more. Nothing has changed except I feel more upset, more vulnerable than ever, and all I hear from Silverman is that's great news. It means all this therapy is working. Great, how come I still feel lousy? He appreciated the family talk video. He said it was helpful. I'm not sure how. I've kept going because it's a routine, and routines make me feel safe and help me cope, but still. This next visit with Doctor Silverman I have decided will be my last appointment.

It's the Friday of the two days I meet with Doctor Silverman, and I am ready to tell him I want to stop seeing him. I've marshaled my reasons in my head, lining them up for when he tries to talk me out of it. I don't feel like this is working out for me and my family. The results are not at all what I was expecting. And frankly, I am fucking tired.

I am in the kitchen by the door, and I ask Barney.

"What do you think about me stopping?"

He sneezes, wagging his tail, thinking, are we going out now? I swear I could read his mind.

"No, dummy, I want to stop seeing my therapist. What do you think?"

He double sneezes again, turns in a circle.

"OK, dummy, here's a snack. We can walk when I come home, OK?"

I throw the snack and he runs, skipping on the wood floors as I run the other way. He will figure it all out in a couple of minutes and do what he does best. He will go to his corner and rest until someone comes home. My love for him and for all my pets – Brandy, Brutus and now Barney – is boundless.

*

The big parking lot off Northern Boulevard is full, since it's a Friday. I park the car, noticing how hot the weather is already, not even hitting summer yet but close. I walk in and there is my trusted doorman. I swear, is he the only one that works here? I wave and smile and make my way to the back of the lobby to the right. It just struck me that here and the laundromat have the same areas I must go to, to get things done in my life. To the back and to the right. Strange how that correlates.

I open the door to the office and make myself comfortable. The routine has become just as if I were coming home. I see the clock says 11:14 a.m. and I go to sit on my ass. The door opens.

"Nicholas, faithfully always on time. Come in."

I make myself comfortable in front of his desk, smiling at the doctor.

"Hello, Doctor. I think that I am done with these proceedings, and I want to thank you for all you have done. I have made enough progress with your help, and I finally feel comfortable with myself."

I see him stop writing and put his pen down. He decides to smile and look at me. I line my supporting arguments up, ready to let fly.

"Nicholas, that's great. I am glad you're all better, cured, and you're hoping to stop. Let me say it's because of all these months of examples and stories from the past that we've aired. We discussed them and you think – no, wait – you believe you're cured, right?"

I agree with him, bewildered. I begin to suspect I might not be using my arguments. I look away. I know that whatever he comes back with, it will be different to any answer I was expecting. And I am right.

He sits forward, so I know he's about to explain something.

"Nicholas, let me just say that if you are so-called cured then you will be the first ever to my knowledge to have achieved that."

I stare at him.

"So what have we been doing all these months?"

"What we've been doing is getting you to the point in our sessions that I call 'The Start'."

I want to say something but there is just too much confusion in my head for me to settle on any one coherent sentence. He seems to hear every one of the questions I'm trying to ask, and he answers them all at once with a question of his own.

"What did I tell you the very first time we met?"

"You told me..." Shit, it's so long ago. "You told me I would never change. But you said you would help me take control of my feelings."

"And that is what we've done. We've got you to the point

where you can begin to do that. But that's not a cure."

I say to him, "What the hell are you talking about?"

"Nicholas, if you would like to stop, it's fine with me, I never push anyone into anything, especially therapy. Would you like to hear my point of view?"

I look at him and say, "Sure."

"Nicholas, there is never a cure in my line of work. People come in here thinking that and when I started, I used to tell that to my patients, until a good, wise old therapist told me to stop doing it. Now I wait to hear what you just told me today, and I explain to the patient how finally they are ready to start the process. Nick, excuse me, Nicholas I'm sorry to say that you will never find a cure for what was served to you, because there is no cure for being abused. You can say it's not fair, what you endured, and I am truly sorry about that. But once you have gone through the abuse there is no way to rescind those memories, those feelings you have inside. How can someone unwatch something on TV or unsee a movie? Memories don't work like that. I'm here with my skills to help you first recognize this whole concept, and you have reached that level. That is so important. There is no right or wrong time. It happens to everyone differently. But now you're there, now it is time to start finding ways or processes or even medications, in some cases, to help you live with these memories and thoughts. And more importantly, not to let your abuse interfere with your life today. In these eight months in therapy you have achieved great results but if you are asking me if you're cured or done, my friend, you're just beginning. The Start."

*

I walk to my car feeling like I did the first day. I feel like a zombie in the parking lot. Once I am sitting in the car I cannot remember walking to it from the doctor's office just a few minutes ago.

I turn on the car, blasting the air conditioning, it's so fucking hot. I grab the steering wheel and yell so loudly. That's all I do, yell so hard. Yell so loudly. Over and over and over. And over.

*

I drive home. I park the car and walk into the kitchen. Barney runs back and forth. Not saying a word, we both go for our walk. It is so hot, but I walk still like a zombie. Barney and I get home. Put all the things away and make our way up to my bed. I put the AC on in the house for the first time for the season. Barney goes to his favorite spot on the bed and I hit my head on the pillow.

If anyone asked me for any memory from the doctor's office, I could not give an answer. I fall asleep feeling the same way I did just as if it was eight months ago, the first day I started.

CHAPTER 33

"... and no cure. He said, there's no cure."

I study the faces of my family, trying to make out what they make of this.

I woke up to a smiling face looking down at me. Amelia, shaking me gently to tell me dinner is ready and the kids are home too.

I told her I was just so tired and that maybe we could eat tomorrow as a family. She kept smiling but I could see the disappointment in her eyes, always trying to hide her feelings. She said, "Sure," and tucked me in better in bed.

Barney decided to abandon me for food. He jumped down to Amelia's feet as she called him and trotted out after her. I just shook my head.

"That mongrel would give up anything or anybody for food!"

But as I was lying there, and my family were eating dinner without me, it occurred to me that I did owe them an explanation. That morning, I had been determined to give up on going to see Doctor Silverman – and I would have broken it to them this evening. Now, after what he said, I am damned sure I'm not going back – so, don't they still deserve that explanation?

I threw back the covers and went out.

I might have ranted and railed for, what, five minutes? I don't know. I do know I got a lot off my chest, maybe a little more than the good doctor actually said. But I certainly got the operative points. My therapist, for whom I have been scraping myself raw for eight months, says there is no cure.

I give them time to digest it. Amelia is the first to speak.

"Honey, hasn't he always said that? I mean, I thought that's what you said he said, right at the start."

He might have said exactly that but I'm not prepared to start cutting him slack, even if it's deserved.

"I guess," I say, and before she can get in with any follow-up remark, I press on, "but I heard it as – no, there's no cure, no turning back the clock, but there will still be some kind of endpoint, some moment where the memories are maybe there if I really think about them, but the effects are, like, negligible. But what he said? The memories will always be there, as fresh now as they ever have been..."

Fortunately the emotions get so strong that my tongue ties up and the words stop coming, which gives Daniel a chance to speak.

"Dad... We want you to be better..." I look at him. "... But we don't care if there's no actual cure! We want to enjoy living with you and feeling safe – and we are! I mean, things really have gotten better over the last eight months. For us. Slightly." He laughs, trying to make it a joke. "I mean, Miranda is still living at home!"

Miranda's mouth barely curls into a smile.

"But you're on notice, I'm seriously considering leaving

again if there's never going to be any change," she says.

"There will be change," I promise.

There has to be. Whatever Doctor Silverman said.

*

I'm still thinking about what Doctor Silverman said today in our session as I lie in bed with Amelia beside me. He told me I have taken a large leap into better mental health, and I still feel lousy. How is that possible?

I stare up at the ceiling, trying to make sense of all this. Things just seem so bad, but I decide to give it another shot with tomorrow's visit to Doctor Silverman. Our Saturday appointment.

*

As usual I arrive on time and make my way into his office right at 11:10 a.m. Like clockwork his door opens at 11:14 a.m.

"Nicholas, welcome, please come in."

I walk in slowly and make my way to my favorite chair. We speak a bit about this and that and then finally I abruptly bring up what we spoke about yesterday.

"I thought you might dwell on that. All day yesterday, and all night, right up until today's visit – am I right?"

He knows darn well he is.

"Please, Nicholas, I want you to believe that you're making great strides here at our appointments. We are now at a point where I can start teaching you great ideas, strategies you can use whenever you encounter a problem."

I stare out the window, thinking about what the hell he just said.

"You need to come to some sort of compromise, let's say an agreement with your brain and your body. You need to understand that your mind has been branded by those unfortunate days of being abused. I really believe that you have reached that point, that you finally get the fact that you cannot be cured, not in the way you may think or want to be. Everyone travels the journey in different ways but to be able to adjust oneself, because there are no cures, one must arrive at this point of control so that triggers in our natural day-to-day lives will not allow ourselves to become an abuser. So, now we are at the point of learning techniques to help with your relationships, especially with your wife and children."

I keep on looking out the window.

"Let me give you some images and words you could use when you find yourself in those moments when your abuse is catching up on you."

I listen intently.

"It's called REBT, Rational Emotive Behavior Therapy, whereby the conflicted person has his whole day mentally planned in advance, with the reactions he will need to get through it already in place in his mind. So then, he can call upon that plan to get through the situation."

"Plan it?" I say. One thing I have never done is plan. I have always let my abuse sneak up on me out of nowhere and bite me on the ass. He nods.

"Back when you had your office job, I expect you sketched out your days, your weeks, in advance, right? So you knew what to expect and what might come up and how to deal with it. I'm sure your wife does the same in her job. One thing you should do now is to create a plan for your daily routines. I want you to draw an imaginary date planner in your head, so as not to fall into any traps that get sprung on you."

I actually think this is a clever idea. I find myself nodding, shaking my head up and down at this first breakthrough, a workable solution in helping with my mental health. For the first time in a very long time, there is a glimmer – it may be faint, but a glimmer – of hope.

"Okay," I say slowly, "I'll draw up a planner for the day as soon as I wake up in bed."

"Yes, as soon as," he agrees. "Use pen and paper to write down your plans for the day, and what might come up, and the remedies you will use if needed. Don't let anything take you by surprise."

Already I'm thinking of everything I need to do to finish a full day, and the possibilities of who I will meet and what things could possibly happen to me. We talk a bit more about remedies and actions to put in place, and for some reason, Bertha comes to mind. I guess this is what she meant – that if I am feeling good with myself and feeling no sorrow then the sessions are not working.

It makes a lot of sense. I know that I still have an uphill battle on my hands but finally with just this one visit, for the first time I feel that I am reaching the summit. I really think this may work.

CHAPTER 34

*F*AGGOT.

I jolt awake, breathing heavily, sweat all over my body. What a fucking dream.

I look around the room and see Barney sleeping soundly right next to me. Did I shout? Amelia's not here and no sound from anyone else in the house. It's still only the afternoon. So, no one to overhear me. Trying to catch my breath I flip my legs over and land my feet onto the bedroom floor.

Still in shock, I wipe my face and rub the back of my neck. My face fills my hands.

"Why?" I keep saying to myself. Why did I go through all this shit? What the fuck did I do to deserve this shit in my life? The doctor wants me to wake up from a dream like that and make a list of which things to avoid saying or doing? Is he for real at a hundred and seventy five dollars a session?

I glance back at Barney, still asleep, snoring like a pig and lying on his back. I think how lucky he is to have such a wonderful life, to fall asleep and reflect on all the love he receives while I am stuck with these fucking memories that come back to me in dreams now – or should I say, nightmares?

*

The events in my dream happened exactly as they did in real life more than forty years ago. It started with me entering my last high school class of the day. Seventh period Italian class. I always sat in the seat right next to the exit door of the classroom to leave quickly each day. Leave the classroom and leave the school building. If I could get out fast enough, I would avoid bullying from the students who just needed to see me now for it to start. Little did I know the plan was already made and it was already working perfectly.

As I made my quick escape out of the classroom, as soon as the bell rang, walking quickly down the hall to the exit, I noticed students laugh and point at me. It only happened when I passed them by, not as I was approaching them, so I didn't think much of it. All I wanted to do was leave the school building and walk home. It wasn't far enough to have bussing, but I think now that was a blessing since bus journeys both ways would probably have been hell rides.

I kept walking and even when I was outside, people pointed and laughed at me, even complete strangers – but only when I passed them. And still I had no reason for why everyone acted this way. I finally made it home and locked the door. I was so happy that I made it home after a whole day without any bullying. I went to my bedroom, put my books away and got ready for my piano teacher to come over for my lessons for the week. I heard the doorbell ring and let him in.

We went to the den where the piano was. I got ready with the music sheets and he pulled his chair up next to my piano bench. We sat down together but I saw the confused look on his face. Then he reached behind me and I felt him slowly peel something off my back. I immediately realized it was a piece of paper, and if that was so then it must say something. I tried to look at what he was doing but he managed to take it off without me seeing what it said. He got up and went into the kitchen, and through the door I saw him looking for the bin. He found it and came back to sit next to me and we continued with the lesson. I spent the entire lesson thinking about what the sign might have said. It must have been nasty, since he gave a nervous laugh when I asked and told me, "It's nothing, please don't worry, forget it."

We had a great lesson, since I enjoyed learning the piano, but my mind could not stop thinking about the sign. When the lesson was over, I walked him to the door, thanked him, told him we would meet at the same time next week. He agreed and walked out to his car. You could see what a nice person he was at heart, because I saw pity in his eyes.

I loathed that pity. I don't know why but when people wanted to help or felt bad for me, I got upset with them. Very stupid of me.

I locked the door and ran to the garbage. I grabbed the sign and read the one word written boldly on it. Then I ripped it up into small pieces, I mean *really* small pieces so no family members would be able to find or read it. I ran to my bedroom, locked the door and fell onto my bed. I just lay there, looking up at the ceiling. Just staring, glaring, not even noticing a tear rolling down my cheek.

I remember that day clearly and the only thing I can think of today is, why did one eye tear up and not both?

And then the worst part of this story hit me with full force.

I went back over that day forensically in my mind, closing my eyes, and I remembered exactly how it all went down, from when I entered the classroom and sat down in the escape chair. I remembered a group of kids talking, laughing, giggling and just being happy to be with friends in a classroom. A luxury I was not permitted in my high school years.

The worst part. The class started. I was sitting there with this student, who I sat next to every day in class. I thought he at least was a friend. He always was kind of friendly. I guess that's why they thought of him as the one to do it. I hoped he was coaxed into it and did not volunteer.

To this day I don't know how they got him, but I remember him patting my back in a friendly way. I took it like a handshake. I remember feeling happy, thinking finally I had a chance to have a friend.

The sign he helped stick to my back said FAGGOT. In nice big bold letters.

*

Now this fucking doctor wants me to wake up each day and make a mental note to react a certain way if I start to act in an aggressive manner? Is that what Doctor Silverman wants me to do? I continue to breathe heavily and sweat harder. I wipe my face with my hands, and now I hear the sound of people entering the house. Amelia, Dan and Miranda have all come home and I try to gather myself and my thoughts, to try and act normal with my family. At least I know what not to do when I see my family, so I guess that is a blessing from my therapy sessions. I am prepared, I have resources to call upon.

I gather up some thoughts, mental notes, and make a full list in my head. I guess finally this is how to handle my life correctly. I make plans so that if one of my family members triggers something in me that takes me back to the days of abuse, I will have a response ready instead of just reacting abusively. I think of consciously making sure not to be cranky or show nastiness. That if they hit my back or rub it, I will not let that simple gesture of caring on my family's part make me think of that kid who pulled that stunt on me.

For some reason I suddenly remember that he was Jewish, so in their minds we occupied similar spaces at the bottom of the heap. Another reason I thought he might be a friend. Weird – didn't Nicholas tell me a story about a kid like that in his own class?

I get myself ready to get up and join my family for a nice Saturday evening gathering with Barney. I make myself presentable, concentrating on this new way of thinking, focusing on the mental notes needed to help me tonight not to bully my family.

"Come, Barney, let's go see everyone."

As I am walking out of my room the door frame triggers one last memory from that episode. What happened the next day in Italian class, over forty years ago. It is still so vivid, so clear in my thoughts. The frame makes me think of the classroom door and, for a split second, I just see empty desks.

I went into the classroom the next day and found the same scenario as the day before. All the familiar groups were gathered in their usual clusters, being sociable and happy. As usual I sat at the desk nearest the exit. The second bell rang, meaning that transferring classrooms should be finished and everyone should take their seats. I sat there, looking around, and the kid that I thought I had a shot at maybe becoming a friend, the kid that to this day I don't know if he was coaxed into bullying or volunteered, glanced at me like I didn't exist. He grabbed his books and went to sit in a new seat away from me and my desk.

I looked at the desk in front, the one behind me and the one to my right side. They were all empty. To my left was the door. No one wanted to sit next to me.

CHAPTER 35

"And as I was walking out of my bedroom, with just a blink of my eyes I saw the empty chairs in that classroom."

Doctor Silverman office, Friday's appointment, 11:45 a.m. He had asked me, "So, Nicholas, how did your week go? Did you start the new process we discussed on Saturday?"

And so I glared at him and started to tell him about the wonderful nightmare that I had during a nap after our session last Saturday.

There is a thick silence in the room, a big elephant right there between us while I try to hold back as best I can from something that happened forty-four years ago. And then I collapse and let go a fury of tears. I get up and pace around the room, weeping, touching picture frames on the walls that are not lined up right. Putting things neatly, setting things up better in his office.

"That's some nightmare, right?" I smile, wipe my nose with a clean tissue from one of the boxes strategically put around his office. I cough and use the back of my hands to wipe my eyes. "That's some story, right, Doctor? I can't make these things up, you know. I was trapped in those classes four years in a row with no means of escape. And now you want me to think back to the things that happened and put them on this mental list so as not to become abusive or act out my anger on my family and friends, right?"

We stare at each other for what seems to be forever, when probably just thirty seconds elapse. Then he clicks his pen, positions it over his pad, and asks some more specific questions about that incident from forty-four years ago. He asks and I answer honestly. We talk like this for some minutes.

I realize two things are happening. I'm able to talk without starting to well up. And...

"Doctor, for the first time, you're actually looking shocked!"

I can see in his face how appalling my stories are to listen to. He pauses, then purses his lips and nods with a smile as though I've caught him out.

"You are quite possibly the worst case I've known," he admits. He is totally transparent about it. I think this event has thrown even him out. For a moment he looks like even he thinks he doesn't actually know what to do to help me cope, although he wouldn't admit that.

"I see you're still upset, even after forty-four years, and I can see that it still affects you in a very bad way. Please understand that none of these events were any fault of yours. We must get you to really believe and understand that."

"Oh, I do." I go back and sit down. "I've concluded that it was my destiny, that life was preset for me to live."

He looks a lot more pleased than you would think, for a man who has just heard his patient say he is fated to suffer.

"That is great! It's kind of like you're forgiving those moments in your life. You're able to grant absolution. You're in a way forgiving yourself. You're bringing those moments to the forefront of your life..." He holds clenched fists in front of them, then spreads his fingers wide. "... And letting them go. Nicholas, that is such a breakthrough."

I say, "Really? Well, I don't feel it. I feel worse. I feel like I'm in mourning. Like someone died and I just finished with all the funeral business."

"Exactly! And what do people do after all the funeral business is over? They move on with their lives. You have taken a remarkable step forward. Now that you have totally accepted your past experiences, you are ready to move on in therapy."

We talk some more about how to do this. He still wants me to start this mental listing of things, either with pen and paper, or just mentally in my head. It must be as soon as I wake up each day.

"Let's go back to what you just told me – the boy who stuck that thing on you. What precise effect has it had on you?"

I think hard. Precise effect? I blow up and hurt people. That's what effect all my abuse had on me.

But I think further, and I guess I can blow up in different ways.

"Okay," I say. "After the note was stuck on my back, when my piano teacher removed it, I suppose a good few years had to pass before I could feel comfortable with anyone giving me a pat on my back. Even when I was in college, I'd finally made it out of school, I was actually making friends and there was another guy who was just happy I joined him and a couple of girls for lunch... And he patted me on the back, because that's what people do, right? And I'll never forget, as soon as I could I went into the bathroom to see if they put something there. That's how nuts I was about pats on my back after that incident."

"Okay." He nods. "So, you note on your list that you might get a touch on your back. It's an extremely common form of social interaction, after all. And that way you prepare for it, so it doesn't catch you out when it happens and you don't lash out by reflex."

Now he's helped me take the first step, I find it easier to come up with more examples.

"I've told you the things that have happened to me in public restrooms. I guess going into one of them is also a pretty common thing each day, right?"

He smiles. "Right."

"Well, when I go into public stalls, even today, I look behind to make sure there is no one walking behind me, ready to jump me. That's fucked up, right? After forty-four years I still can't take a piss without being afraid. Wow!"

I'm running in my head through a normal day in the life of Nick Rato. In the life of any ordinary American male, which technically, legally, externally is what I am. Now that he's given me eyes to see, I'm seeing traps everywhere in the most everyday things.

"This is a good one. Say I hear any loud public announcement – of people cheering or booing or anything – it could be anything, yelling about a politician or at a game, anything where words are being shouted – I feel it's at me. Because I've been yelled at in public too. Mean, humiliating things just shouted at me by other kids while their parents just looked on, not doing anything."

"That certainly goes on the list," he agrees. "Chances are good you'll hear something like that every day."

We end our session and promise to speak some more about this the next morning, Saturday, at 11:15 a.m.

Walking to my car is different today. No more zombie in the car park. I can't explain exactly what I feel, just that I don't feel disgusted anymore. I feel like I just finished some type of medical procedure and now I am in the recovery room, to rest and get my body, mind, and soul back to its old self again. Like the quiet time that comes after a thunderstorm. That quiet time that occurs after any big event, whether it be positive or negative.

From my family's point of view, I might as well be on a different planet that evening. My thoughts certainly aren't with them. All day my thoughts have been circulating around me. I've been peering into them, trying to make things out, and slowly but surely, patterns have been emerging. New realizations and understandings flowing out of what Doctor Silverman has said.

And then I think, *Wow!*, as it hits me.

*

I arrive at Doctor Silverman's office for Saturday's appointment and for the first time we both sit looking directly at each other. I tell him straight.

"You remember I wanted to know, *why?* Why this abuse occurred? I've realized it will never be answered. It can never have a rational answer because there is no answer. I searched high and low for an answer to that question – but it's just rhetorical. Isn't it? So I can stop looking and – well, and get on. I'm a work in progress. A work in progress for the rest of my life."

For the first time in a long time a smile, a real smile comes over my face.

CHAPTER 36

As usual, on laundry day my family have everything ready for me to bring to the laundromat. I arrive and find the place empty – apart from one small figure sitting at the back right side, just where I'm headed.

Nicholas lifts his head as I come near. His eyes are still dark and hurting but somehow I see them differently now. Because I guess I know now there is hope, for him and for me.

He starts like we're already halfway through a conversation.

"Once, I was in a room, an empty classroom waiting for a teacher. I don't remember which but we three kids were just waiting. The other two were playing volleyball with a globe of the teacher's. They both just acted rowdy as I just sat waiting. Then another teacher, Mrs Malloy, she saw what was happening from the hall and came in yelling, what were we three doing? I swear, I just sat looking forward, hoping they wouldn't touch me. Anyway, she said that our teacher probably wasn't coming back but we three got detention at end of the day. I swear, I had just sat waiting. Anyway, we went to detention and as we went in, those two kids put on their angel faces, one of them even cried, said they did nothing and they didn't know why Mrs Malloy gave them detention. The teacher doing detention listened and said for them to go home, not to worry. I sat in detention for two hours, okay, with many other kids too but how unfair is it that those kids got away with murder? And then I went home and my mom found out, and I got a severe punishment from her because I embarrassed the family by getting detention. So, I didn't do anything, those rotten kids did..."

And we both say together, "... they got away and I suffered in school and at home," finishing the sentence in perfect unison. We look at each other. Okay, that was weird.

What's also weird, well, unusual, is the effect that Nicholas's story is having on me. It isn't. In the past he's told me about something happening to him, and it's injected poison right into my soul and I've gone home and poisoned the lives of everyone around me.

But now they're just words. I know what they mean to him, and I cannot and will not deny his experience and his pain. But thanks to Doctor Silverman, I now know how to take charge of my feelings.

I try to spread the joy. I open my mouth and he speaks first.

"If you keep seeing that man, I can't see you again."

"That's my business, Nicholas," I say gently.

He glares at me.

"He can't make you better."

"No, and he never said he could. But he can make me better to live with, not a danger to my family. I'll take that."

I want to help him, but I'm not going to let him control my actions and I'm certainly not going to be blackmailed by a kid. So I take charge of the situation by getting up and starting the load running. When I look around, he's gone.

I hear loud laughter coming from the manager's office, and there's a cloud of smoke floating in the air around the door. I look inside and I see Bertha and her sister Blanche, folding clothes and talking. They see me and in unison they say, "Hey, good morning!"

"Hello," I say back, and then there is a silence that lingers, and I just don't know why.

Bertha starts. "So, how is our favorite doctor doing? You still seeing him?"

I start to answer her, and Blanche says, "Bert, you know not to just ask private questions? You especially should know that – *duh!* Don't you remember when you needed help?"

I say, "It's okay. After all, your sister's the one who suggested I start seeing Doctor Silverman in the first place."

Bertha says to her sister, "You hear that? Be quiet and let the man talk. Go ahead, honey."

I start to tell them both, "Well, he's really helped me with the biggest obstacle in my way..." and this time Bertha interrupts.

"The 'why' thing, right?"

I look at her in disbelief and wonder how she knew what I was thinking. Bertha goes on.

"Do you know how many people say, why me, why me? We all have it in our heads, like we own it, and the same answer applies to all of us too. I even think Blanche tells herself that 'why' crap too. Right, sis?"

Her sister replies, "Yes!" They laugh hard and blow their smoke in my face.

Bertha invites me with a gesture. "Say, Mac, take a seat."

"I need to check my wash."

"Sit down!" she tells me again. Then, to her sister, "Please, take care of the man's clothes in the washer."

Blanche answers, "Hey, I'm here on a visit, not to work!"

Bertha smiles and yells, "Bitch, get back there and finish the man's laundry! Please?"

Blanche goes out to check on my loads, but gives a wave with a pronounced middle finger waving in the air.

Bertha grabs a chair and sits right in front of me.

"So, you worked out that the 'why' thing is the same B.S. for us all."

Bertha's sister yells from the back, "Hey, his clothes are all done. How does he want this to dry?"

"Put it all in the dryer is fine, thank you," I call. I look at Bertha. "The worst part is how I ruined so many other people's lives. All that abuse I went through ruined me as a father and a husband. My abuse only lasted four years but there seems to be no end to it."

There is a big silence in the room. We just sit there looking at each other until Blanche yells from the back, "Am I done back here? I got nothing to do but watch his underwear go round?"

Bertha yells, "Get your ass back here, and stop looking at his underwear!"

I ask Bertha, "If I may, what happened to you that you needed to see Doctor Silverman?"

Bertha looks at me and sits up straight in her chair. She takes a deep drag from her cigarette, exhales it.

"Let's just say I wasn't in the mood for love but a strange

man that saw me was. Funny, we both went to prison. We both got a twenty-year sentence. Nick – is that your name? – I thought what happened was my fault, I deserved it because I was too stupid or did the wrong things. The only wrong thing I did was thinking in that way. You, me, and the others out there that bad things happen to, we got to yell to the world that we did nothing to deserve what we got. And sure as hell we got to stop letting these people who ruined our lives back then – they must not ruin our lives now. Or in the future." She smiles at me, touches my chin. "Let's go see what Blanche is doing to your clothes."

She starts to go, and then she stops and puts her hand to her head.

"You've got me going, Nick. I was almost back into the old ways of thinking, that way again of 'why me?' thoughts and going back into that prison. So once again, I'm deciding not to be anyone's abused victim. You'll be amazed how often you have to make that decision. You need to stop being a prisoner of your *own* making."

*

They both help gather up all my laundry. We all three hug and go back to living our lives, and as I walk away from them, a great fog of smoke engulfs me. I just smile, shake my head laughing and walk out of the laundromat. I get into my car and make my way home.

I get all the stuff out of the car and make my way into the house via the kitchen back door. As usual, Barney runs to the kitchen door with one of his dolls, ready to play. Running in circles, back and forth until he realizes that I am getting his dog leash. Then his whole world changes because he now knows it's time for his walk. Walking time is his favorite part of the day. No matter what weather is out there he is ready.

On the way home, I could not stop thinking of what Bertha just said: "Stop being a prisoner of your *own* making." This plus realizing there is not an answer to "why?" are the two great breakthroughs I need to continue my journey towards ending this existence that I have gotten so used to living.

I decide to make a call to leave a message on Doctor Silverman's voicemail. It is about 3:30 p.m. and I am sure he's busy meeting with one of his clients.

*

"And please leave a short, detailed message including your full name, date of birth, your reachable phone number, and a brief description of why you have called. Doctor Silverman will get back to you within twenty-four hours."

BEEP.

Coughing and clearing my throat, I am just about to start my message when I look up and see a mirror facing me. A mirror I never noticed we had here in the kitchen.

"Doctor Silverman, it's Nick Rato..."

I cough and clear my throat again but can't help looking at my image in the mirror. I see something I have never seen before. I finally see a man fully aware and confident. A man with the self-control and determination to end this journey once and for all.

In fact, it finally dawns on me that I always had control

over when to move on. I alone control the happiness in my life. Time wasting and thinking of time wasting is ruining and wasting more time. That all must stop right now, today!

I continue my message.

"I just had another great breakthrough and get this, it was with Bertha. Yes, Bertha, our lady manager of the laundromat. What you said today, plus my talk with Bertha, finally made me realize all the great things you've been waiting for me to get. You know I've realized there's no cure, and there's no why – and I see I have a chronic condition that I will have to work on for the rest of my life. And now I realize I've been a prisoner."

The mirror shows me a man who finally realizes that he was the only one who was holding the key that locked himself into this life of abuse, this so-called jail.

"So, I'm setting myself free."

CHAPTER 37

The obstacles that blocked my view of my future have finally been removed. I have never felt so liberated as I feel today. All those demons have been scraped off my back and their claws unclenched from my shoulders. All that weight has been lifted from my body and for the very first time I have a path to follow. A path filled with all the types of situations that may occur to any of us. But that's the wonder of living. I feel that any situation, negative or positive, I will be able to handle it.

There's one important ground rule. I know now that from time to time, life circumstances will arise and I still may get triggers that spiral me back down to self-pity and abusive behavior. But now I am at least aware that triggers may occur, and I am ready with the REBT doctrine Doctor Silverman has introduced to me. So, this will be a lifelong situation, knowing I need to stay proactively aware.

The only way I can find a happy life is through my own decisions to live a happy life. Whether life decides to share with me a bad outcome or a great one, I know I will be able to deal with it.

*

My cell phone rings ten minutes after I left my message for Doctor Silverman. To my surprise I see it is him, calling me back. I didn't ask him to return my call so why is he calling? This whole year, I don't remember ever speaking to him on the phone except at the very beginning when we first started our sessions.

Anyway, I answer my phone.

"Hello, Doctor Silverman, how are you?"

"*I am doing well.*"

He sounds like he's doing very well. I remember the first time I heard his voice on the phone. Detached and professional, offering his services, take it or leave it. But now... He sounds happy.

"*I just finished with one appointment and as I'm waiting for the next, I always check my messages. I got your message and was delighted to hear what you had to say. I think back to when we started a year ago...*"

I say, "It's been a year? I guess time does fly."

Doctor Silverman says, "*I just want to say that you really have come a long way in understanding how this system works, and how it works for each of us in a different way. I'm glad to continue our sessions and I feel that you're now ready to start having an appointment once a week. We can meet Fridays at 11:15 a.m. Does that suit you?*"

I take a second to answer. I know he wouldn't try to talk me out of it if I wanted to end our acquaintance now. But one thing I have learned is to trust his opinion. I will continue to see Doctor Silverman for as long as he thinks is necessary.

"That suits me fine, Doctor... And looking back now, I am truly happy my washing machine broke down last year."

There is a baffled pause, and then I hear him say, "*I beg*

your pardon?"

I laugh out loud and explain to him the chain of events which led me to his office. My washer breaking down, going to the laundromat, meeting Bertha, and suffering through her smoking fits, and leading to her recommending his services. Understanding, he begins to laugh as well.

I tell him, "I'm a firm believer that there are pathways in our lives that are predestined, and they happen for reasons unknown to us, but they act in our best interests."

Doctor Silverman says, *"Hmm. I'm not too sure I agree with that type of thinking but I certainly can see why some of us feel that way. You were given a difficult path in life, but I can honestly say you are working your way back. I believe things will eventually seem easier, and better to cope with in the future. My next appointment is here, we can talk more on Friday."*

I reply, "Have a great day, Doctor Silverman, and see you on Friday."

We both hang up, chuckling. He goes to open the door for his next client while I close a door to a past life.

CHAPTER 38

Snores were coming through the door. Miranda waited, her hand raised, her knuckles just brushing the wood, and she could swear she could feel the vibration.

It wasn't Dad. It was Barney, the cute little dog napping with him and snoring like a big fat pig. She never could understand how a small dog could snore that loud. And if you woke him up to stop, he looked at you with dazed eyes, and then went right back to bed not caring what you thought.

But she wasn't going to let the household's smallest and cutest member get in the way of what she wanted to do. The day had come and she wasn't going to be put off. She knocked as a courtesy, and went in regardless.

"Hi, sweetie!" Her father sounded surprised, like someone just receiving an honored guest. He rubbed his eyes and pushed himself up on his elbows, wiggled into a sitting position. "Come and sit."

Barney struggled to his feet and came towards her, tail wagging, Miranda hesitated, then pushed Barney's dolly aside and sat down where it had been. This would have been so much easier if it had gone as she had planned. If she had just stood over him and spoken her prepared thoughts.

Well, she could do that now, even from a sitting position.

Except that, it turned out, she couldn't. She opened her mouth, and the words just would not come.

The silence grew deafening, until with a touch of his hand on hers, he started.

"Miranda, my darling, let me say this to you. You and your brother have never done anything for me to have treated you like I have, the way that has made you so upset. I own this completely and one hundred percent take responsibility for my actions. I wish, sweetheart, I could go back and change what I did, how I ruined so many years for you and your brother, but I can't. But, I can see the present and I can look to our future to lead a better life. I can do that for you and Dan. Please know you did nothing to be given the childhood you went through."

And just like that, she was undone. The carefully prepared phrases evaporated, the devastating put-downs melted to nothing, and the storm of emotions below them burst out. It was a waterfall of pent-up anger and resentment that she finally let go and which spilled out in the form of uncontrollable tears. She fell into his arms and howled into his shoulder.

"Why? Why, Dad? Why did you act like that towards us all? It didn't matter how happy or nice I felt, you were always so tough and mean. It's like there was a funeral in the house every single day."

"Why?" he murmured, while he gently patted and rubbed her back, and for some reason she sensed the question amused him, like it had some extra meaning only he knew. But it didn't mean he didn't take her seriously. "Yes, my darling, you're so right, but it is so important now that you understand you did nothing to deserve it. It was all my fault, and I am hoping, no wait, I am *making* sure our future will be different. You know I suffered many years of abuse myself but I am not making excuses about why I acted so poorly. That was all on me. I understand I am guilty for the way I've acted in this house all these years."

The sobs were dying down and they pulled gently apart. He swung his legs over to get up and fetch a box of tissues for her. He put them on the bed next to her and Barney lifted his head up just to look at the box, hoping it was food, but it wasn't, so he put down his head again on Miranda's lap. Miranda pulled a tissue from the box and blew her nose.

"I see you're trying to make amends," she sniffled. "I want you to know that I have noticed it all this year – I've seen you talk better and smile more. You try to make us all happy and I see you're trying to control your yelling. And so I want to believe that I can do this and have a good relationship with you. I just don't know if I can do this so late in the game."

It was so weird how he didn't even try to dodge it. She remembered his reaction when she told him she blocked his number – the hurt, the incredulity and then the anger that he tried unsuccessfully to hide. But apparently this was Dad v2 and he just sat there and took it.

"I completely understand, honey. If that is how you feel then I have to accept you feeling that way. One thing I can promise you, though, is I will try to make up for all this lost time. Can you at least try and give me a chance to show you?"

No.

Yes.

Somehow both answers were on the tip of her tongue at the

same time and she didn't want to open her mouth in case the wrong one came out. The result was another deafening silence.

But she knew which one she wanted, and suddenly she was afraid she might still say the wrong thing. She wiped her eyes again, to give herself time to get her thoughts together and make sure she said exactly what she meant to say.

"Yes, Dad," she said carefully, "that is something I could do."

And despite the changes in him, she could tell he was glad. "Thank you, sweetheart."

She smiled back.

"You know I came in here ready for a battle? Ready to tell you I was going to tell you off and cut you out of my life?"

"What changed?"

"The way you didn't give me excuses and try to dodge the responsibility. It all changed the minute you took full responsibility for your actions. How could I disown you when you were owning up? I couldn't do that."

"Then I am so grateful we talked," he said, warmly and sincerely, with his own eyes brimming. "I have a lot to make up for."

"Yeah." She couldn't quite give in to her urge to fling her arms around his neck. Play it cool, girl. "You get another chance."

But however hard she tried to play it down, she couldn't stop the corners of her mouth from curling upwards as she said it.

"I won't take it lightly," he promised.

"I will leave one day," she added. "But it will be for the

right reasons. Me growing up and moving on. I'm almost there now. But I won't just be fleeing."

"That works for me, honey."

He started to lie back down, which was like a cue to leave, a high note to end the conversation. But first she leaned over and gently kissed his cheek.

Barney looked up as she stood.

"You wondering where I'm going, hey?" she asked lightly. Barney looked at her, then at Dad, who shrugged.

"I have no answers for you, Barney. I just have hope."

Barney put his head down on the bed and waggled his tail. Dad looked up at her and smiled again.

"I take that as a good sign!"

CHAPTER 39

My cousin Tony's big smile takes up the screen. "You're telling me that, Cuz? That is so great!"

There's not so much more to say. I only need to give him the latest news, not the background. He knows that because he was there at the start, even before Amelia and the kids. I wonder if he realizes how important he is to me, how important he always was, especially over those horrible years. We were living thirteen hundred miles apart and the telephone was my only comfort back in those days. I would call him and tell him all these things that happened to me, and he never broke my confidence. Never a word did he speak to anyone about the abuse. He never used it for gossip or petty talk. I come from a very judgmental, gossiping, make-fun-of-people-type family but he never joined in those types of antics. He never laughed or used my dad's kind of argument – "What kind of a man are you? You're a sissy, a momma's boy, you're a faggot, grow up, be a man."

Instead he tried his best to comfort me. He was almost two years younger than me and had to be the grown-up on the phone as I poured out my heart and soul. Looking back now, I am amazed how well he handled it and provided words of wisdom.

I consider Tony to be my best friend and a brother-type figure, even though he is my cousin. I had always wished that we were truly brothers, but nature chose this path again for me. It doesn't matter because I got the last laugh again on destiny. I feel closer to Tony than anyone else in my life besides my wife and children.

Knowing Tony, he would say something like, "That's how it should be. I'm supposed to be number four in your life." I hope he knows today how much I truly love him.

There was a time, after three years of abuse, that I wanted to run away from home, and I told him so. I even shared my plans, such as they were, which wasn't much. He never belittled me or spoke down to me, which is what people will usually do to try and get you to change your mind from doing something crazy, like running away. He even helped me plan my escape. He knew the best way to handle the situation was by working with me but always trying to lead me not to do it, in a way that wouldn't make me say, "Oh yeah, well, I'll show you all I can make it out there with no one helping me."

"Think about it, Nick, maybe you should postpone and wait for this month?" Or, "Look, why not wait until you can save more money and then leave?"

I look back and marvel at how courageous he was, knowing what to say even at his young age, and risking the fact that I might still go and do something stupid. We always got off the phone having pushed back my departure by a few more days. All his efforts worked because whenever the time came, I postponed to a point where I never did leave. I hope he knows how truly grateful I am for all his efforts to help me. He was two years younger than me and acted better than most men I knew back then and even today.

"So, what are you all doing to celebrate?" Tony asks. "Going out to a nice restaurant?" I shake my head.

"I made dinner," I say. "A nice meatloaf with potatoes and salad." He laughs.

"Of course! A family favorite!"

It is, as well as very appealing to Barney. I try to find small, dry bits of pieces mixed in with his regular meal plan. The meatloaf is a nice extra bonus in his bowl.

It was a pleasant family gathering – good food and people daring to enjoy each other's company. I was pleased to see Miranda less anxious and more like herself. She has a wonderful, fun personality that can usually bring good spirits into a room. Meanwhile my son is just like his mom, always with less to say but still leaving an indelible mark on you when leaving the room. I barely noticed my food as I sat there admiring each one of their remarkable ways and characters. I feel so blessed to be surrounded by them and I thank God every day I have them in my life.

Yes, of course, I feel that way for Barney too. I have so much to be thankful for and am extremely lucky to have them all in my life. How stupid that it took me so long to grasp that. It is never too late to see and believe. That really is true.

Tony and I finish our chat and I fold the laptop shut. Then I look at all the different programs I may watch tonight. I hear Barney coming to my bedroom, so I call him. He waits patiently till someone comes up behind to pick him up and put him on to the bed, so that's what I do. Amelia soon follows and we start to watch one of our favorite shows. I guess we all fall asleep because I wake up in the middle of the night. I see it is 2 a.m. and turn the TV and lights off. I fix the covers so Amelia will be warm; the seasons are changing again. Fall is back in full swing with the cold air upon us. You can feel it standing next to the window.

I pass the time waiting for sleep to claim me by running through a list in my head. People who need to be told what has happened to me. Amelia, the kids, Doctor Silverman, Bertha, her sister, Tony even Barney... check, check, check.

There's one last guy in my life that I need to see, but I've never known how to get hold of him.

CHAPTER 40

I was looking out my window at a terrible rainstorm, and tears rolled down my cheeks as the rain lashed against the window outside. I wiped my eyes and turned to look at my clock radio. I had woken up before it had a chance to switch on. Everyone else in the house was asleep still. I was the only one up that early, getting ready to go to my first day in college.

Graduating from high school had felt like a release from prison, an innocent man found guilty of not being up to the standards of a human being at the ages of 14–18. My jurors were an entire school of teenagers and the judges were all the adults in my life who turned a blind eye to the facts of the case. They passed judgment that it was all my fault. I was found guilty in everyone's eyes, and sentenced, and now my sentence was up.

And so I was crying because that was the only way to mark this transition in my life. The first day of freedom.

I went into my bathroom and did exactly what I had done the last four years of my life. Prepared myself to be clean and neat. Wear proper clothing, leave my home. Now the only difference was I had my own car. I drove to the new school, a private small college in my hometown. My parents had made it quite clear that they wouldn't support me if I left home and went to a dorm-type school. I was told firmly to get that out of my mind. They had already wasted three years of money paying for a private high school. So, I made my way to college in this rainstorm and arrived promptly for my first class at 8 a.m. in the morning. It was still raining hard as I parked my car. Other students were also parking up and dashing through the rain to the building, trying to get to their 8 a.m. class as little wet as possible. It was a college math course, one of my required classes to take in the next four years.

I ran through the rain myself and into my first class. I dried myself off and instinctively looked all the way to the back of the classroom for the last chair. The class was full and I wanted to make sure, as I did in high school, to have no one sit behind me.

While I got myself settled, a student to my right said casually, "Hey, some storm out there, right? Where I come from, we never have storms like that. Wild, right?"

I was in shock. I looked both ways, thinking to myself, "Is he talking to me?"

I answered, "Um, yeah, right, it's real nasty, the weather."

I went back to getting myself together, and he came back again with another question.

"Are you from the area? I'm from North Carolina. Hey, I'm Scott. We never get storms like this in my hometown."

I was still fixing myself, putting books not to be used in this class on the floor and taking the books I needed and putting them on my desk. Then this girl in front of Scott's desk turned to say hello, and then the girl in the front of my desk turned to jump into the conversation. It was like I started to hear them all talk as I was floating above us four, looking down, thinking, "Are they talking to me as if I had comments to contribute?"

I floated back into my body when Scott said that I was a native and asked me more questions. He told the other two girls, who were also out of state students, that I probably could answer any questions better than him. The three of them looked at me and I asked, "What was that again?" They laughed and smiled and one of them said, "He is zoning out already!"

I answered their questions about the area and they were still being friendly. As the teacher came in, the girl in the front of me said, "Let's grab something later and you can tell us more. Can we all meet like around 11:45?"

Funny, I swear I remember that time, 11:45 a.m., even today almost forty years later. We all agreed and were all in the student lounge by noon. We all got to know a little more about each other. The three of them had smooth conversations while I gave one-word answers.

We stayed about an hour, and they thanked me for my help and said, "See you Wednesday in class." I smiled as we all departed and went our separate ways. Scott patted my shoulder hard, saying, "Great meeting you, bro."

He took off. I looked around, like, what's going on here? People are not avoiding me. In fact, they include me, *me, ME!* They wanted to know my feelings and they wanted to know my opinions. I looked around at people of all walks of life, walking around, smiling, saying hello to me, yes, *me*. This cannot be true. I mean, what's going on here?

And then, of course, I had to go to the bathroom and check my back in the mirror. Just in case he had stuck something there. He hadn't.

It was a good day. A great day. And days like this turned into weeks that turned into months that turned into years. It had all stopped. The ridiculing, the meanness, the smacks to my head, the trips from behind to make me fall.

But all I could think at that time was that damn word, *why?* *WHYYYYYYYYYYYYY!*

*

I open my eyes and I'm back, today, sitting on the park bench at 6 a.m. walking Barney.

"Well, boy, ready to go home to Mom, Daniel and Miranda?"

He sneezes, his way of saying yes. I look around at this beautiful brisk fall day coming to life. Time just goes on whether you like it or not. It caters only to itself. It has no master and pushes us all, ready or not. There is not one thing, as humans, we can do to stop it.

I get up. Barney looks up at me and starts walking happily towards the house.

So, I still think about *why?* The infamous word that followed me all my life and especially this year in my sessions with my therapist. But now I know there's no answer, it no longer torments me, I can look at it analytically. Just at that moment, without me noticing, a jogger runs by.

"Hey, Mr. Rato, hi, Barney." It takes me a moment to recognize the young man, because he is one of Dan's friends and I don't get to meet many of them. He is showing respect and being cordial. Like Scott and the girls. Like normal people, reaching out because that is what people do, and I can answer in kind.

"Hi there!" He has jogged on before I need to remember his name, which is just as well. I blow into my hands and say to Barney, "It really is quite cold today, right, Barns?" Barney doesn't even look up. He is on a mission to get home, into his warm home, into my wife's morning hug.

How much time did I waste, thinking, *why?* Time that could have been used for me as a person, a son, a brother, a friend, a husband and as a father. A father: that was the most important part of my life, and I wasted that time.

I like to think the world is safe, made up of good people. I realize it is not always a wonderful place. Our lives have a purpose on Earth and whether the results are favorable or not we need to fulfill our role. I know it's wrong and not fair at times but that's the way life has been set up for all of us. I know the bad things that happened to me weren't my fault but what was my fault was how I reacted to them. I must live with that too, now. I know it is never too late to understand this and change myself.

I hate the fact that bullying still exists, and now thanks to technology, bullies today have found even more imaginative ways to hurt their victims, who are all inducted into a club membership no one applies for. No need to lurk behind them or wait for them outside of school. The internet has made the problem exponentially larger, with results too horrible to even think about, like self-inflicting harm to the point of suicide, with no near clear insight for stopping it. Why, why hasn't the world realized how bullying has gotten so much worse, and why –

there, that word again – why as humans haven't we cured the problem? A sickness that doesn't need medication, a miracle cure. And yet mankind still cannot manage to cure a simple disease like bullying. How sad that we live in a world where we spend billions and billions of dollars on technological advancements and yet have no cure for seeing meanness right in front of one's eyes. Whether we see it physically in front of us or on the network, cyberbullying, we are still turning away and saying, "Not my problem." Why? Yes, the simple three letter word, why? Why isn't there an answer to 'why?'

*

"Well, Barney, here's the house. Should we go in?" Barney sneezes hard, which is a definite answer to get our asses inside. I let go of his leash so he can run ahead. I turn around and take one more glance behind at this beautiful, cold fall morning. Knowing all too well nothing has changed in the world these last forty years – except that now, no one has power over my life. I learned this year that I am the only one with that power. I must rely only on myself. I am happy if I want to be happy.

I stride into the kitchen where my family are stumbling into wakefulness and a new day, and they glare at me as if resenting my energy. I hold my arms out wide and beam at them.

"It's time to order that new washing machine!"

"It's about time!" Miranda snarks.

CHAPTER 41

The machine arrives today, and so I won't be going back to the laundromat. Well, maybe for old time's sake, but I've learned not to hang on to the past.

But what with everything, I at least owe Bertha a goodbye.

I back the car out of the garage, twist my head left and right to check I can reverse safely out into the road.

While my head is over to the left, I hear the passenger door open. I look around just in time to see Nicholas climb in. He sits down and fastens his seat belt. Then he just looks at me. I look back.

"I wondered if you'd come," I say.

He seems taller, older. Well, he is. It's what boys his age do when you don't see them for a while. I remember Daniel. Monday, still a cute pre-teen. Friday, taller than me with a voice like a concrete mixer.

"Can you drive me to work?" he asks.

Instead of the usual t-shirt and jeans, he's wearing an ironed white shirt with a colorful logo on the breast – a waffle cone overflowing with bright pink ice cream and sprinkles – and a neat little paper hat.

Ah, yes.

"Sure," I say, and as I put the car into "drive", I think I know which particular item he is going to draw from the bottomless pit of nightmares.

*

"I don't care, I just want him gone!"

Nicholas paused, his hand on the door. Mr. and Mrs. Albert, the married couple that ran the shop, were arguing at the front of the store. Nicholas was in the back room, and he could hear every word.

Nicholas had moved on from the concession stand. Now he worked at Mister Ice Cream, the park's ice cream parlor. He usually slipped in at the back door so that he could put on his apron and hat and appear fresh and ready at the front to serve the public. Going in at the back also had the advantage of being a more direct route. He could usually get in there without being seen, avoid any ambushes that might be laid for him – and when he traveled in his mom's car, he was even more protected.

The Alberts didn't know he was here. This was awkward, and embarrassing, and hurtful because it was obviously about him. And also kind of weird because he usually got on OK with Mrs. Albert. He didn't get to see Mr. Albert much, but she always spoke about him in a nice way. Now, even back here there was a tension in the air that triggered his every survival instinct and made him just want to get out.

He peeked out the back door – just in time to see the rear lights of his mom's car disappear round the bend. So, he was stranded in the back with the argument at the front.

He deliberately shuffled his feet on the floor and pushed

the door shut hard enough to make it slam, because the last thing he wanted was for them to find out by accident he was here. They might think he had been spying on them, ears flapping like an elephant.

But still they obviously didn't hear because they kept on. Mrs. Albert was trying to be the voice of reason.

"Honey, you just don't know..."

He talked right over the top of her.

"That fuckin' kid, the freak with all them pimples and fuckin' big nose, he has to go. We are losing a fortune on cakes when he's working."

Nicholas closed his eyes, groaned silently, rested his head against the cool tiles of the wall.

They had found out.

Mr. Albert's voice dropped half an octave, trying to meet her reason halfway.

"Look, hon, just do the sums. The cakes we get through, profits should be way up. But we're losing, and guess what, we lose every time *he's* on the night shift."

Ice cream cakes were disappearing from Mister Ice Cream in a way that didn't register on the cash till. What else were they supposed to think?

Nicholas could have told them exactly what to think, but that would have meant snitching, and then his life would be even less worth living. Easier to stay in one place, ride the wave of goodwill until the bullies caught up with him again and it was time to move on.

Part of Nicholas's job was to clean up and close up at 9 p.m. He was usually here on his own. And the bullies knew it.

They lurked outside. He could see them gathering like wolves. He tried to stay at the front, but there were always inevitable moments he had to go through to the back, and even if it was only for thirty seconds, they swooped in and took a cake. Or two. Or three. They were easy pickings, kept up front in the parlor.

It had taken him some time to notice, to work it out. They came in when he was on his own behind the counter, and of course he had to serve them. At first they had been almost civilized and he had even thought they might be treating him with more respect, now that he had something they wanted – the ability to dispense ice cream, or to withhold it. They would pay up for their purchases. Under protest, and exaggeratedly counting out their dollars and cents like they were at kindergarten just learning to count, but still. They did it.

Then they would hang about outside the parlor and eat their purchases. Rather, eat their acquisitions. They were hamming it up, waiting for him to notice that they were eating more than he had sold them.

That had been the beginning. But soon they grew bored of jumping through the hoops to at least try and make it look legal. So they just started taking stuff regardless.

They still ate it outside. Pushing it into their mouths, goggling eyes at him, taunting him.

And Mr. Albert thought it was Nicholas doing it.

And now Nicholas knew what Mr. Albert thought of him. He thought so little that he couldn't even say his name.

"That fuckin' kid…"

Nicholas squared his shoulders, tied the strings on his apron at his waist, settled his hat on his head and pushed his way through to the front room. The argument stopped in mid syllable and they stared at him in shock.

"Good afternoon, Mr. Albert, Mrs. Albert. I'm here."

He met their gaze levelly, giving nothing away. The way they looked at him – him with blatant dislike, even her with suspicion. But they couldn't make themselves say that they had just been talking about him.

"*That fuckin' kid, the freak with all them pimples and fuckin' big nose.*"

He knew now. That was all he meant to Mr. Albert.

It would be so much easier just to say his name. Nicholas.

But you couldn't say that with quite so much expression of how you really felt.

*

"Nicholas," I say, "I know. Remember, I've been there. I've been exactly there."

"So you know there's no way out."

"I know there's no way of ending the bullying, because there's no reason for it in the first place..." I start to say, and he interrupts.

"Of course there is. It's me. I'm at fault. It's just in my nature. It's who I am."

"It is *not*," I say firmly. "You are not guilty in any way. Any way at all. You're not at fault for any of the stuff that happens to you, and these years do not need to define the rest of your life. But, things will not change unless you take charge of your life and look for help. That means, professional help outside your own family. I get that you want to keep it inside the circle – I know, Italian families, right? – but I know the circle you have and I know they can't handle it. I also know you want to hug it close to you and suffer because it's just so darned humiliating to have to tell anyone about it. You think the long term pain is worth the short term pain of opening up. But, the longer you wait, thinking things will get better, that things will work out themselves, the harder it will be."

Nicholas just stares ahead, not knowing what to say. Lights ahead are just changing to red, so we slow down and stop. For a while Nicholas and I just sit there, waiting for them to change. Eventually we move off again.

"You have a whole life ahead of you, kid, but you have to find a way to get control back of it. It's never too late to do this, and the sooner the better, not only for your own life but for all the people who love you. That includes people you don't even know exist yet. Your wife, the kids you will one day have. You will truly be taken by surprise, how much you love them. At your age you can't imagine laying down your life for anyone, but trust me, when these strangers come along into your life, suddenly overnight you would die for them if it was the only way to protect them from other people. But as for yourself, if you don't change it now then you will end up hurting them more than you can imagine."

He so desperately needs to understand. Everyone needs an identity, and teenagers more than anyone else as their brains rewire themselves into their adult personas. An identity is a teenager's most precious commodity, and this one would rather hang on to what he has – flawed though it is – than surrender it for the unknown. For the mystery that lies beyond his therapist's door.

"But there's one more thing," I say. I tap my head gently. "You can know all this, up here..." And then I thump my chest, over my heart. "But you have to believe it here. You can't just do this with head knowledge. That might be how you start off, why you start to get help in the first place, but this is a whole new way of thinking and the change will only happen when you believe it with all your heart, body and soul."

The last turn into the laundromat parking lot is coming up. I indicate and slow down.

"Do you get that, Nicholas?"

I look at him briefly as I say it, and I see the first signs of a smile, but there's another car coming towards us and I need to let it pass before I can go ahead. So, I'm not looking at him as I speak.

"It's never too late, but you have to understand this, body and soul. You have to let this understanding change you. Will you do that?"

There's no answer, just something changing inside the car. Certainly no door opens or closes. But the next time I look at the passenger seat, the belt is still done up but otherwise it's empty.

A breakthrough has taken place in a small little Lexus, while traffic whizzes past us on the highway. This day has been far too long coming and has wasted far too many people's lives as well as Nicholas's own.

But Nicholas has his own life now.

*

Bertha is delighted. She throws her arms around me and hugs me like she wants to crack my ribs, and she tells me not to be a stranger. We are both damp eyed as I head home.

I look forward to going home, to seeing my darling wife Amelia and hugging Barney, making him feel safe and loved. I will only look forward from now on. I will never look back again, and I will never allow the world or the time we live in to take control of my life away from me, ever again.

I get home, park up, go through the door into the kitchen. Barney is playing with one of his favorite toys. Amelia is chopping stuff at the counter. She looks up with a bright smile. It is still such a novelty to see my family look at me without any shields up, shutters behind the eyes poised to come crashing down. My own eyes prickle slightly.

"Nick," Amelia says, "Buy Brands called, and they will be here around 10 a.m. to deliver the new washer and dryer. Will you be ready?"

My smile splits my face in two, as I say with all my might, "Yes, I am ready!"

THE END

DEAR READER,

I hope you have enjoyed this raw and honest account of the life I experienced from the ages of 14-17. Maybe "enjoy" is the wrong word. I mean more that I hope the book was a success in opening your mind to the true results of "harmless antics of high school youth experiences." The person experiencing those antics suffers so much harm, and they have the rest of their life to struggle with the aftereffects – for themselves, and especially for the people around them.

Those "harmless antics" ruled my life for the next forty years, in a very bad way. My reactions to many of the trivial things that we all go through in life were unreasonable, way out of control, and they began to ruin the life experiences of the people around me. They were a clear result of the abuse I endured. I walked this Earth with a force inside me that ruled my everyday life and decision making, and my children, especially my daughter, truly suffered from how I acted. Four years of abuse ruined forty years of my life, and as I have said, time doesn't care. It doesn't stop for anyone or anything. It continues on its own. So, please, if you take away anything from this book, it is that you can never get back the time you waste.

Being in therapy helped me understand many things. It made me see that I can't be cured and that I will have to live all my life with the memories of abuse. They will never go away. And it helped me see that I will never have an answer to the question of why this happened to me. Finally grasping these two facts is the solution to my mental health. Now, when certain thoughts are triggered by everyday life situations, I am able to react in the correct manner to adjust to the situation. I still sometimes go back, revert to old habits of reacting, but I can honestly say my life has changed 90 percent in a favorable way. My wife, children and friends all see a big difference in my attitude and my way of life.

So, from this book, take away the satisfaction of finding your own "Doctor Silverman" and getting back control of your life, instead of the abusive behavior having control over you. And remember, there will never be a cure. It is something you need to work on every day of your life.

Please feel free to email me any questions you may have at **www.nickrato.com/contact** or **nickratowrites@gmail.com**. I will try to get back to you in a timely manner. Look towards the future, thinking that this too can be controlled, but make sure you get the correct help.

If you're a parent and you see this happening to your child, please immediately take appropriate action. And make sure you let them know that they do not deserve this treatment in any way. Make sure they understand that it is not their fault. Not their fault. Not their fault. Reiterate that message each day to them.

All my best,

Nick Rato